JUS

How sad, Joss thought, to feel funny and strange around Fletcher, of all people. Ever since Joss had moved to Massachusetts six years ago, she and Fletcher had been inseparable. But now they were both thirteen, and Joss had started shooting up and filling out, while Fletcher, lately, was always making atrocious dirty puns, and practically foamed at the mouth whenever he saw a pretty girl. Joss didn't want anything about their friendship to change – but maybe some change was inevitable.

She had plenty of other things on her mind without Fletcher bugging her. Her father's job at Bronwyn University was up for tenure this year, so he was pretty grouchy these days, and tough for her and Mom to live with. Joss worried too about what was happening between Dad, so handsome, so charming when he wanted to be, and Phoebe Jackson, the most devoted of his students.

Then at school, there was Twig to preoccupy her. He was the only boy who made Joss feel there might be something to be said for growing up, but whenever he spoke to Joss her IQ seemed to drop about fifty points and words of more than one syllable deserted her. He did act friendly, but perhaps he really preferred the sophisticated Bobo . . . Sometimes Joss wished she'd lived at a time when life was simpler, and there were clear rules about everything . . .

This warm, funny, honest story of a girl starting to grow up should be enjoyed by anyone of about Joss's age.

JUST
GOOD FRIENDS

JANE O'CONNOR

PUFFIN BOOKS

Puffin Books, Penguin Books Ltd, Harmondsworth, Middlesex, England
Viking Penguin Inc., 40 West 23rd Street, New York, New York 10010, U.S.A.
Penguin Books Australia Ltd, Ringwood, Victoria, Australia
Penguin Books Canada Ltd, 2801 John Street, Markham, Ontario, Canada L3R 1B4
Penguin Books (N.Z.) Ltd, 182–190 Wairau Road, Auckland 10, New Zealand

—

First published by Victor Gollancz Ltd 1984
Published in Puffin Books 1986
Reprinted 1987

—

Copyright © Jane O'Connor, 1984
All rights reserved

—

Lines which appear on p. 104 are from the song
'Ballad of a Thin Man' by Bob Dylan
Lines which appear on p. 172 are from the song
'Great Day' by Vincent Youmans

—

Printed and bound in Great Britain by
Cox & Wyman Ltd, Reading

for Jilly

One

"Can you honestly picture your parents doing it?" Fletcher demanded of Jocelyn.

"Shhh!" Joss said, hoping to avoid an answer. "I don't want to miss this part."

They were sprawled on the floor of the Longmans' den, or "library," as it had been called in the house's grander days. The rickety air conditioner was going full blast while they passed a bottle of root beer back and forth and watched an old Peter Sellers movie called *The World of Henry Orient*.

Joss hunched forward, closer to the television, pretending to be deeply engrossed, although how on earth was a person supposed to concentrate when Fletcher kept popping out with questions like that?

It made her so uneasy. Lately all Fletcher wanted to talk about was sex. What percentage of girls did she think were still virgins by the time they graduated from high school? . . . Had Cheryl Carter really gone as far as some of the older boys in tenth grade claimed? . . . Was it true you could catch mono from making out too much? . . . As if Joss had the answers!

Rats! Joss was losing the thread of the movie, just when it had reached the most important part. The teenage heroine, it seemed, had discovered that her mother was having an affair with a famous concert pianist.

"The last thing in the world I can picture is my parents doing it," Fletcher went on after he drained the last of the root beer. "I just can't see them, you know, rolling around, panting and sweating and yelling 'More! More!' They're not the types. Do you know what I mean?"

Yes, Joss confessed to herself that she did. But she refused to admit as much to Fletcher. Instead she sighed an elaborate sigh and assumed a tone of extreme patience. "Of *course* they do it, Fletcher. Everybody who's married does."

Fletcher was eight months younger than Joss and now nearly a full head shorter since she had shot up to an alarming five feet nine. Making him feel juvenile was one of the few weapons Joss had against him.

Fletcher, however, did not appear humbled. "Thank you, Jocelyn. I'm not a total moron," he said.

"I *know* they do it. I just can't imagine it." Fletcher paused for a moment and then laughed. "I bet afterward my father gets out his pipe and tells my mother how they both just shared one of life's most meaningful experiences."

Joss couldn't help laughing now, too. Dr. Dwoskin, who was the psychiatrist at Bronwyn College for Women, was a firm believer in meaningful experiences. Of all kinds. Last summer, for example, Fletcher had been shipped off to a Vermont farm for a meaningful rural experience. It lasted exactly three days. The chickens gave him asthma.

Joss gazed with sudden fondness at her friend, who was wearing a T-shirt that said "Minus 10" on the front. With his wispy reddish-brown hair, thick horn-rimmed eyeglasses, and frail build, Fletcher looked like the perfect 98-pound weakling.

"You're too much, Fletcher. You really are."

"Thank you, thank you." Fletcher went into his Groucho Marx routine, waggling his eyebrows, puffing on an imaginary cigar, and leering at Joss through his Coke-bottle lenses. "You're not bad yourself . . . if you get my meaning." And in case Joss hadn't, Fletcher outlined the shape of an hourglass with his hands.

Joss tried hard not to wince. She hated for Fletcher to make dumb comments about her body . . . and lately he'd been making lots of them. As if she wasn't self-conscious enough already that she was turning into a teenage Dolly Parton!

3

"All right, Groucho. Time to say *sayonara*," she said as evenly as possible. The worst thing was to let Fletcher know he'd embarrassed you. Then he'd never let up. "Ma's last class isn't over until six, and I promised I'd start dinner."

"I can take a hint." Fletcher got up to leave. "Anyway I have to get home in time for *Lucy*." In the six years Joss had known him, Fletcher had never yet missed an episode.

Joss waved good-bye from the den as Fletcher opened the front door, clutched his throat, and pretended to stagger outside into the shimmering heat. Here it was, only the beginning of April, and the temperature had hit the high eighties for the second day in a row.

Joss dragged the old wicker rocker directly in front of the wheezing air conditioner and tried to concentrate on the rest of the movie. But her mind kept wandering.

What was going on with Fletcher? Lately he was always making atrocious dirty puns, and whenever he saw a pretty girl, he practically started foaming at the mouth. Bobo Wilder called him the Overactive Gland.

It was ridiculous, not to mention embarrassing. If she had any guts, she'd tell him so, straight to his face. Joss scowled. Why was it that she was so afraid of standing up to anyone? To say what she really thought? Fletcher certainly wasn't that way. Just the opposite. He didn't give a flying leap what anybody thought of him.

Absently Joss picked at a hangnail. Fletcher. How sad to feel funny and strange around him, of all people. Her oldest friend in the entire world. Ever since Joss had moved from Manhattan to Higham, Massachusetts, six years ago when Dad had joined the English department at Bronwyn, she and Fletcher had been inseparable.

Their friendship had been cemented one day in second grade when Joss, who even then had a few inches and at least ten pounds on Fletcher, had saved him from getting creamed by Butchy Sullivan in a dodgeball game.

Butchy, who threw harder than anybody in the class, had seen Fletcher trip and was all set to clobber him while he was still on the ground. Fletcher was such a total spaz—always the first one out in any game; always the last one picked for any team. Without even thinking, Joss leaped in between the two of them, crouched over, and took the blow that was meant for Fletcher squarely on the back. That single uncharacteristic act of bravery had won Fletcher's undying loyalty, although lately, more and more, Joss wondered why he still bothered to hang around with her.

It wasn't just that Fletcher was so much smarter—he had an IQ they were still trying to chart. But Fletcher was more inventive, more daring. He could convince Joss to do things she'd never dream of doing

5

on her own. And things always happened when she was with him.

Like the time last summer when they'd gone to the movies in Springfield. They hadn't been in their seats for more than a minute when Joss heard a very familiar aristocratic voice behind her say in a stage whisper, "Really. It never fails. Somehow I always wind up with someone BIG in front of me . . . *Always* get the big ones. Right smack in front of me."

Joss flushed straight to her scalp and tried slinking down in her seat. The woman was talking about *her*.

Fletcher heard, too. "Talk about rude! I ask you. Is it your fault you're overgrown?"

With an outraged glare, Fletcher turned around. Then suddenly his expression changed from one of righteous indignation to one of awe and disbelief.

"Katharine Hepburn!" he bleated. "Katharine Hepburn!"

It was her. The cheekbones, the hair, the voice. It was *her*!

Fletcher scarcely missed a beat. "We wouldn't mind switching rows, would we, Joss?" he suggested. Joss, openmouthed, nodded dumbly.

"Why, really. That's awfully nice!" Katharine Hepburn said in her best Katharine Hepburn voice.

Fletcher placed his hand over his heart. "You're looking at a man who's seen *Stage Door* eleven times," he said with feeling. "I'd do *anything* for you."

That clinched it. After the movies, Katharine Hep-

6

burn treated them to tea. And Fletcher managed to act like a perfect human being the entire time. Not even once did he go into his KH impersonation.

Yes, Fletcher often made life interesting. If only he'd quit acting so weird.

Joss settled back in the rocker and half watched the end of the movie. She'd missed some important stuff, but it looked like the girl's parents had gotten divorced and now she was going to live with her father. Just like Laura Weiss, the new girl from California who'd transferred to their class in February. Laura claimed she was glad her mother had decided to "call it quits," but Joss simply couldn't fathom that.

She heaved herself out of the rocker and clicked off the television. For a second she gazed at the framed photo of Mom and Daddy on top of the set. It had been taken on their wedding day in the middle of Central Park. Daddy had had a beard then. Her mother was wearing granny glasses and her hair, pale nothing brown and stick-straight like Joss' own, had been much longer. They looked so happy, gazing into each other's eyes. The picture of true love. Joss wished they looked that way more often now.

Although she'd listened to it a zillion times, Joss never grew tired of hearing how Mom first met Daddy when she was at Barnard and he was graduating from Columbia. It was so romantic. They'd been at a protest march against the war in Vietnam, and, for Mom at least, it had been love at first sight. A few months later, she dropped out of college to marry Daddy and help support him through grad school. That was why Mom's parents hadn't even come to the wedding. They'd been furious that Mom had given up her education. But if you truly loved someone, then no sacrifice was too great. And of course it was easy to see why Mom had fallen completely head over heels for Daddy. Who wouldn't? Daddy was handsome enough to be a movie star, with his thick dark hair, dark eyes, and crooked smile. Laura even said so. Next to him, Joss felt as if she and Mom just sort of faded away. And Daddy could be awfully charming when he wanted to be. The other night when Laura had come for dinner, Daddy had been in especially good form, telling them about his first girl friend ever.

"Irma Jean Gittelfarb. How's that for a name? But to me it was poetry. She had incredible black hair down to her a—" Daddy stopped, remembering his audience, and took a drag on his cigarette. "Well, down past her waist. I was pretty obnoxious in those days. I always wore this idiotic little felt hat that I thought made me look like Bob Dylan."

"What made Irma Jean like you, then?" Laura inquired.

"Ah," Daddy said, exhaling a curling ribbon of smoke, "Irma Jean loved me for one reason and one reason only . . . I could blow double smoke rings! Watch." Daddy puffed in deeply on his cigarette, pursed his mouth into an O, and formed, first one and then another circle of smoke that drifted together,

8

making an almost perfect figure eight that hovered over the dining table.

Later Laura said to Joss, "I *love* your father. He's terrific. Your mother sure has all the luck." And from her tone Joss could tell that Laura didn't think shy, quiet Mom really merited her good fortune.

Of course, Daddy wasn't the easiest person to get along with. Especially lately. She glanced once more at the photo and then turned toward the kitchen to heat up the meat loaf Mom had left out. Still, Joss supposed that Laura was right. Mom was pretty lucky. After all, hadn't she married her one true love?

Daddy came home in a foul mood that night. To put it mildly.

The minute he walked through the door, he holed himself up in his office and started playing old Beatles and Bob Dylan records until Mom coaxed him out for dinner. That was when he erupted.

"You know what really burns me?" he said, jabbing at a potato with his fork. "If I don't make it, I won't even have the satisfaction of being able to tell myself that I didn't play their little game. Oh no! I've sucked up to all those impossible blowhards. I've kissed their fat old fannies just like everybody else who's up this year."

"Up" meant "up for tenure." This was her father's sixth year as an assistant professor of English, the year the senior members of his department decided whether or not they wanted him for keeps. If they

didn't, he could stay at Bronwyn one more year—
the terminal year, it was ominously called. Then he'd
have to find a teaching job at another college, one
that wouldn't be as good as Bronwyn, probably. But
if Daddy *was* granted tenure, then he'd have it made.
He'd be a member of the Bronwyn faculty forever.

"You mean that if, a few years from now, they decided that they'd made a mistake and you weren't
such a hot teacher after all, they couldn't fire you?"
Joss had asked once incredulously.

"That is correct, Ducks," Daddy had told her.
"When they take you they're stuck with you. It's like
marriage without divorce. Take Cedric Whipple. Now
there's a guy who's got the brain of a paramecium.
He's a prime example of how screwed up the system
is." Professor Whipple was the chairman of the department and had been teaching Chaucer at Bronwyn
since just about the Middle Ages. It was Daddy's the-
ory that Cliff Notes supplied Professor Whipple with
all his lecture material. "Of course, if they do take
me, then I'll think the system reflects the highest standards of scrupulous judgment and fair-mindedness,"
Daddy had joked.

"I figure they've got to take Dixon," Daddy said
now, flicking his ashes into the pyramid of cigarette
butts building in the ashtray beside his plate. "She's
decent and they need more women on the faculty.
And Goldthwaite is a shoo-in. Perfect background.
After all, his father rode crew at Yale with Ceddy
Whipple." Daddy looked disgusted. He took one last

deep drag on his cigarette, then rubbed it out. "It'd be different if times were better. Then maybe they'd take all three of us. But the college is hurting for money. No way can they make that kind of financial commitment."

"But all your students adore you," Mom said with a nervous edge to her voice. The final decisions were made sometime in April. It could be almost any day now, and Mom too was feeling the heat.

"It's true, Daddy. I bet you're the most popular teacher on campus," Joss put in. The times she'd sat in on her father's classes, she'd seen the way the girls hung on his every word. And every year there always seemed to be one girl in particular who'd end up attaching herself to Daddy, dropping by his office all the time or calling him at home to discuss some paper. Last year it had been Andrea Something-or-other, an earnest girl with stringy hair that always looked like it needed washing. But this year it was a senior named Phoebe Jackson who was not only beautiful but evidently brilliant, too.

Joss stole a sideways glance at Mom and sighed to herself. Mom's hair was pinned haphazardly on top of her head with one of Joss' barrettes, and, as usual, she didn't have on a smidge of makeup.

"The faculty knows how popular you are, too," Mom continued. "That's got to count for something. In that last student course critique, you got raves. Nobody else—"

"Oh, for Christ's sake. Do you think it really matters

what goes on in the classroom?" Dad cut Mom off sharply. "You don't know squat. It's all political."

Mom turned pale. Joss stared down at the puddle of gravy congealing on her plate.

"You are so naive. You think it's the same as being a student," Daddy went on. "Do a good job and your paper comes back with an A on it. Well, it doesn't quite work that way."

"All right, then. You're right. I'm wrong. You *won't* get tenure!" That was how Mom always fought with Daddy. By giving up and agreeing with him. Mom set her coffee cup down hard. Then she said, "*Please*. Let's talk about something else. Just for one evening."

A tense quiet settled over the dining room, making it seem even larger and more forlorn-looking than usual.

Joss kept her eyes riveted on one of the somber, faded cabbage roses patterned on the wall facing her and searched for something, *anything*, to say to break the uncomfortable silence.

"So how'd Professor Macdunna like what you wrote for the house tour brochure?" she finally ventured. Her mother was finishing up her degree at Bronwyn now, and had organized the upcoming "Historical Houses of Higham" tour as a senior year project. It seemed a safe enough topic of conversation.

Without warning, Daddy pushed his plate away from him, crumpled his napkin on top of it, and stood up. "That's what's known as an exit line, and I am taking my cue," he barked. "Because if there's one subject I don't feel like discussing, it's Ian Macdunna. I've had it to here"—he pointed to his forehead—"with Ian Macdunna."

Grabbing his pack of Pall Malls, he headed for his office. The door slammed, and a minute or so later the nasal voice of Bob Dylan could be heard coming from the tape deck, twanging out lyrics to one of his long, incomprehensible songs.

Joss and Mom were left alone in the dining room.

Joss fiddled with her napkin. "Hey, Ma, I'm sorry. I didn't mean to set Daddy off like that."

Her mother got up and began scraping dishes, piling silverware on the top plate. She seemed to be avoiding Joss' eyes. "It's not your fault, honey. Don't worry about it."

"But why did he get so ticked when I mentioned the tour and the professor?" Professor Macdunna was Mom's favorite teacher. He was a stout, red-faced man with a thick British accent, and Joss had liked him the couple of times he'd been at their house for dinner. "I guess maybe Daddy is just mad at the world," Joss ventured.

"Maybe so," Mom answered without looking up from the plates she was stacking.

"You just know when this whole thing is over and Daddy has gotten tenure, he'll act like he was sure all along it would work out okay and *we* were the ones who were nervous." Joss made herself laugh as she followed Mom into the kitchen. "Isn't that right? Isn't that just how he'll act, Ma?"

But her mother wasn't taking the bait. She was bustling around the kitchen wrapping remains of the meat loaf in cellophane, scooping leftover salad into a Tupperware dish.

"Hey, Ma, everything will be all right, won't it?" Joss asked with more urgency. Where *would* they end up if they couldn't stay in Higham?

Mom finally looked up from the Tupperware. "I don't know, honey," she said quietly. "I hope so."

That was not the right answer. Ma was supposed to say that of course Daddy would get tenure. But even if he didn't, it wouldn't be so terrible because no matter what happened, they had each other.

"I'll tell you what I do know, though," Mom continued, kissing Joss on the forehead. "I know I love you," and she forced a smile.

Joss smiled back uneasily. It seemed obvious Mom didn't want to talk more. She could get that way. Just clam up on you. And when she was in that kind of mood, forget it. You couldn't get anywhere with her.

"I'm letting these go till later," Mom said briskly, surveying all the dishes stacked methodically in the sink. "I have a paper due."

Joss nodded dumbly and preceded her mother out of the kitchen.

Daddy *will* get tenure, Joss stated emphatically to herself as she climbed the stairs to her room. Then maybe life could settle back to normal. Joss flopped down on her bed. Staring up at the plaster scrollwork of vines and leaves that bordered the ceiling, she listened to the muffled music coming from downstairs and the clatter of Mom's typewriter across the hall.

Once upon a time in the not-too-distant past, the three of them would settle in the cozy den each evening after dinner, to read or study. To Joss the den had always been the true heart of their home. But now every night Mom and Daddy took to separate corners of the house.

Beyond her fluttering curtains hung a fat bluish moon, and for a long time Joss lay staring at it, exhausted but not sleepy. A fly brushed her on the face and continued cruising about the room. By morning there would probably be zillions of them, but Joss couldn't bear the thought of closing the window, and the screens were all the way downstairs in the back of the hall closet.

As soon as the music and typing stop, I'll be able to go to sleep, Joss told herself, but eventually they did and she didn't, and when the house fell dark, settling into its usual chorus of groans and rumblings, she was still wide awake.

Sometimes late at night, the house still gave her the creeps. Neither she nor Daddy had liked it much when they first moved in. "Ridiculously big," Daddy kept complaining, "and pretentious for just three people." Maybe her mother had thought at that time there would be more children to fill up the empty rooms, but none ever came.

Still, in time everyone seemed to grow into the house, and by now they had almost stopped noticing how queer and old it was, with odd cupolas and turrets, peeling gingerbread trim everywhere, and pull chains on all the toilets.

Rubbing her eyes, Joss looked at the relentless glowing hands of her alarm clock. Rats! It was almost twelve thirty. She'd be dead tomorrow. She clamped her eyes shut. Outside something rattled against her windowpane. "I did not hear that," Joss muttered between gritted teeth. "I am falling asleep."

Then it happened again. There was a *ping* at the window, and then whatever it was ricocheted inside, *thunk*ing on the wood floor. With a sigh of surrender, Joss cocked an eye open and sat up. Probably some psychotic squirrel in the giant elm outside.

"Joss," a familiar voice whispered.

Joss went to the window and peered into the darkness. There was Fletcher straddling one of the branches, attempting to look casual while he tried desperately to keep his balance.

"Bon soir," he said with a wave that nearly sent him plummeting.

"Fletcher! For God's sake, what are you doing out there?"

"I'm going swimming."

"Well, be careful. I heard a couple of people have drowned in this tree."

"Very funny," Fletcher said. He blew on his forehead. "I swear it's ninety degrees. I'm going to the Bronwyn pond for a quick dip. Come with me."

"Count me out."

16

"Don't be a killjoy. It'll be fun."

"Yeah, I've heard that one before." Joss waved her hands to ward off further discussion. "Lookit, no way am I sneaking out to go swimming in that slimy pond."

"Then come keep me company," Fletcher wheedled. "It's no fun going alone. . . . And besides, what if something happened to me? You'd never forgive yourself."

Joss paused for a fatal split second. If appealing to her sense of adventure wouldn't work, then appealing to her sense of responsibility was bound to do the trick.

"Oh, for Pete's sake—"

"Good old Joss. I knew you wouldn't let me down." Fletcher beamed from his perch.

"Good old Joss," Joss grumbled to herself as she went into her closet and slipped on a bathing suit under jeans and a T-shirt. It seemed she'd been hearing that all her life. Good old Joss. Loyal Joss. Always-there-when-you-need-her Joss. It made her sound like Lassie.

"Okay, let's went," she said with resignation, hoisting herself out the window and into the tree, which she shimmied down with ease. Huffing, Fletcher plopped to the ground beside her, and together they slunk down Willow Street.

"What happens if we get caught?"

"Your problem, Jocelyn, is that you're too law-abiding."

"My problem is I let you talk me into doing dumb stuff."

"Well, don't worry. The campus cops only go on patrol once an hour, on the half hour. They won't drive past the pond until way after we're gone."

Joss did not bother to ask how Fletcher knew this. He always had access to inside dope.

They walked the rest of the way in silence, Joss soaking in the calm quiet of the night. Shredded bits of cloud veiled the moon, and the long branches of the giant willows, which stood at the edge of the pond, dipped and trailed in the water. Joss' spirits began to lift. It was so beautiful out here. So romantic. The only thing spoiling the picture, Joss thought with a giggle, was Fletcher himself, sporting an Alfred E. Neuman T-shirt and baggy Bermudas.

"Last one in et cetera, et cetera." Fletcher was busily adjusting his nose plug. A second later he splashed into the water and dog-paddled toward the island in the middle of the pond. Never Never Land. That's what they'd called it when they were little.

Peeling off her shirt and jeans, Joss tentatively sank a toe into the soft, squishy bottom and gazed out to the island. The tops of the pine trees looked sharp enough to burst the big balloon of a moon. In the inky water Fletcher was flailing around, kicking up a storm. By now he was halfway there, and he turned around, impatiently motioning for Joss to join him.

Well, why not? she thought, and took the plunge. She always seemed to be following Fletcher some-

18

where. At times Joss felt she was no more than a convenient sidekick. Fletcher had her around the way the Lone Ranger had Tonto. Or Lucy had Ethel Mertz. How pathetic!

When she reached the shore, Joss ran up and splashed Fletcher, who was sitting down, his head cocked to one side, knocking water out of his ears.

"Hey, cut that out!"

"Make me." Joss scooped up more muddy water and doused him again.

Fletcher jumped up. "Okay, you asked for it," he hollered, and tore off after her.

A slurpy mudball went sailing past Joss. Then—*splat!*—one landed on the back of her leg. Joss turned, caught another on the shoulder, but managed to score one on Fletcher before he raced up and came in for the kill.

Grabbing her in a death lock, Fletcher rubbed a heaping handful of mud into her hair.

"Enough! Enough!" Joss pleaded, laughing, surprised at how strong his hold was. Mud ran down her face and into her mouth. She tried to squirm away, clutching the top of her suit to keep it from slipping down.

"Sorry. Can't hear you." Fletcher continued his shampooing.

"No more, please. I give up," Joss gasped.

Suddenly Fletcher let up. His face was very close to hers. They were practically nose to nose. He stared intently at Joss, and for a split second she had the crazy thought that Fletcher might try to kiss her. Then he loosened his grip, and Joss broke away. Still panting, she threw herself into the water to rinse off and then collapsed on the grass.

Fletcher plopped down beside her, looking immensely pleased with himself. "I guess that'll teach you not to mess with the kid," he crowed. "But next time don't expect me to show any mer—" In mid-sentence, Fletcher stopped short. His eyes bugged out, and his mouth fell open.

At first, when Joss turned to follow his gaze, all she caught sight of was a beached canoe and two paddles lying in the sand. Then, quite a bit further back, behind some scrub bushes, she began to make out a tangle of arms and legs. Two heads bobbed up.

"Relax," the guy said to his date. "It's just a couple of kids."

The girl, who looked like she probably went to Bronwyn, laughed nervously as she disentangled herself from their pretzel-like embrace. She patted her hair and straightened her skirt.

"Please, don't let us disturb you," Fletcher called out in his most polite tone. "Just go right back to whatever you were doing. Pretend we're not here."

"Fletch-*er*!" Joss poked him with her elbow.

"Listen, you little wise guy. You have no business being out here." The guy was wagging an accusatory finger at them. "So why don't you just beat it. Now."

"Well, ex-cuuuuuse me," Fletcher sang tauntingly. "C'mon," he said to Joss. "I guess we know when we're not wanted."

Then, before Joss could even put together what was happening, Fletcher had raced over to the canoe and was struggling to push it into the water.

"Hey, wait a minute," the guy hollered. "What do you think you're—"

"Bye-bye, Romeo!" Fletcher called out. "Wish us *bon voyage.*

"Help me, dammit," he ordered Joss, handing her a paddle. She obeyed, and they shoved off while the guy and girl, frantically waving and shouting, became smaller and smaller figures on the island.

"Did you see the look on that guy's face?" Joss said as they glided through the water in their hijacked canoe. "Talk about homicidal!" She burst out laughing. "Fletcher, I've got to hand it to you. This was definitely one of your better moves."

"Thanks, kid. That means a lot to me."

"Did anybody ever tell you that you do a rotten impersonation of Humphrey Bogart?" Joss said fondly as they beached their canoe by the college boathouse.

Ten minutes later they were back at the side entrance of Joss' house, having successfully eluded the Bronwyn campus police.

"I'm glad you made me come," Joss whispered. "See you tomorrow."

"Yes, nothing beats a romantic moonlit dip. Too

bad it wasn't with Twig Lorimer instead of yours truly, huh?"

"Fletcher!" Joss said in exasperation. "Don't start with that again. For the forty millionth time, I . . . do . . . not . . . like . . . him." Joss enunciated each word slowly, but she did not sound terribly convincing, even to herself.

"Okay, okay, forget I said it." Fletcher got his bike and wheeled it down the driveway. Then he mounted his fancy ten-speeder, called out softly, "Heigh ho, Silver. Away!" and pedaled off into the night. Joss watched him disappear around the corner before she sneaked inside.

Slowly, very slowly, she turned the knob on the creaky back door.

The bright light in the kitchen took her by surprise.

"Joss!" Mom yelped, and backed away, startled, from the wall phone where she'd been standing.

"Ma. Hi!" Joss half waved and smiled sheepishly. She was dripping on the floor. "Fancy meeting you here."

"Jocelyn! You gave me heart failure." Mom sank down into a kitchen chair and pulled her old terry cloth robe around her. "What in God's name are you doing soaking wet at one thirty in the morning?"

"Don't get upset, Ma. Fletcher and I just went swimming at the pond. It's such a hot night, and I couldn't sleep anyway."

"Fletcher. Who else." Mom's face softened, and

she smiled grudgingly. "Swimming in the pond, huh? Well, I suppose that's not a federal offense."

"Then you're not mad?"

"No. I'm not mad." Mom looked tired. She brushed away a strand of pale hair that had fallen from the barrette. "Who knows. If I'd been asked, I might have gone along, too."

"Next time, Ma. Next time."

Mom gave her an affectionate swat on the can. "Now you scoot upstairs this minute, miss. Get yourself cleaned up and dried off. You're a mess. And *be quiet.* Your father just went to sleep a little while ago, and he's grouchy enough lately without you waking him up."

"I won't make a sound, Ma. I promise," Joss said, and together, arm in arm, she and Mom mounted the stairs.

While she was towel-drying her hair, Joss congratulated herself for having wound up with Mom for a mother. What if she'd gotten stuck with a flake like Mrs. Dwoskin, or, worse, someone like Laura Weiss' mother who had just up and left her family one day?

It was well after two by the time Joss crawled back into her old-fashioned spool bed, the one Mom had discovered at a tag sale and had painstakingly stripped down to its original pine wood. Only then, as Joss dipped into sleep, did a faintly disquieting thought dart across her mind. What on earth had her mother been doing by the kitchen phone at that time of night?

Two

Miss Kasper was letting them have art class, the last period of the day, outside. Joss grabbed the woodblock she was working on and hurried to her favorite spot, a huge cherry tree exploding with fluffy popcorn blossoms, which overlooked the pond and the Bronwyn campus.

Fletcher flopped down beside her with his sketch pad, and a minute later Laura Weiss joined them, so that they formed an almost perfect equilateral triangle under the tree. Laura ripped off the top sheet of her sketch pad and placed it beneath her. "So I won't get grass stains on my skirt," she explained. "It's brand-new."

Laura had more clothes than anybody in the world.

Today she had on shocking pink culottes, a shocking pink blouse, and shocking pink espadrilles.

"Ooh, smell the air. I still can't get over how there's no smog in New England." Laura sighed contentedly. "It was nice of Miss Kasper to let us outside."

"Big deal," Fletcher said. "When Kasper told us she had a treat, I thought maybe it was something exciting . . . like a nude model."

Bobo Wilder, who was sitting nearby, looked up from the collage she was making. "Honestly, Fletcher," she said. "You are such a child."

Michelle Kline was sprawled on the grass next to Bobo. She emitted a soft, condescending snort and added, "Yeah, Fletcher. Isn't it about time to grow up?"

Michelle was harmless enough, Joss supposed, only it was pretty pathetic the way she copied everything Bobo did. If Bobo tried a new hairstyle, Michelle would do hers the same way. When Bobo went skiing over Christmas vacation, Michelle got her parents to take her to the same place. Last fall after Bobo fractured her arm roller-skating, Joss had half-expected Michelle to show up with a cast, too.

"Oh, you mean girls," Fletcher exclaimed in an injured falsetto. "Why don't you go and pick on someone your own size?"

Joss and Laura laughed. That was Fletcher for you, making fun of himself before anybody else had a chance to.

"Listen, will you all kindly lower it?"

Twig had said that. He was stretched out in the sun, a few feet away, his sketch pad shading his face. "Some people are trying to work."

Smiling, Joss glanced up from her woodcut and allowed herself a brief, longing look at Twig, all five feet, ten inches of him.

What exactly made Twig seem so special, Joss wondered, besides the fact that he was the only boy in their class who did not make her feel like the Jolly Green Giant? Of course he was a Lorimer, and that in itself was intriguing, Joss had to admit.

As a rule, Lorimers did not attend public school. Twig had gone to Higham Country Day before he went to some boarding school in Vermont. The rumor was he had flunked out and was spending this year at their school before his parents shipped him off to another prep school.

"Well, what should I try my spastic hand at today?" Fletcher was now saying to no one in particular.

"If you want, you can draw me," Laura suggested to Fletcher. "Just as long as it's not in profile." Laura had a big nose, but she wasn't particularly sensitive about it.

"Class, less talking and more drawing," Miss Kasper advised as she wandered among her students. She stopped behind Jocelyn and squatted down, peering over her shoulder. "That's a very interesting design you're making with those letters."

Joss smiled.

"HHH. What does it stand for?"

"Historical Houses of Higham. There's a tour a week from Sunday. My mother sort of planned the whole thing, and I'm designing this letterhead for her brochure." Joss said the last part softly. In a way she felt funny about helping out Ma. It seemed kind of babyish. Kind of nerdy.

"Yes, I think I read about the tour in the paper," said Miss Kasper. "Isn't the Lorimer house on it?"

"Yes. . . . Ours is, too," Joss said. "I live in the old Mortimer place."

"Oh, isn't that the house where—"

"The mayor choked to death on a wishbone." Joss finished Miss Kasper's sentence for her and nodded. That incident had secured a permanent, if rather odd, place for their house in local history.

"I remember old Miss Mortimer," Miss Kasper went on to say. "She always went around in farmer's overalls and tennis shoes with the toes cut out . . . even in winter. That house, though, was supposed to have been the last word in fancy at one time."

"Yes, I know," said Joss. She knew because there was a diary of Millicent Mortimer's in the house, which she'd read more times than she could count. "Professor Macdunna told us that the house is a classic example of Victorian kitsch."

"You don't say!" Inexplicably Miss Kasper burst out laughing. Then she said, "Well, I'll be certain to come by, Joss. And I want to remind the class, too." Miss Kasper stood up and clapped for attention. "Kids, I want to make sure you know all about the historical house tour on April . . . fourteenth." Miss Kasper looked at Joss to confirm the date. "Professor Ian Macdunna, who is a very famous art historian from Oxford and who is teaching at Bronwyn just this year, will be giving a lecture next Thursday night at the college. It's open to the whole town and he'll be talking about . . ."

Joss tuned out the rest of what Miss Kasper was saying. It embarrassed her the way so many kids were rolling their eyes and making faces. Poor Mom. If she could only see the reactions.

Joss concentrated harder on her woodcut. It was especially tricky scooping out the bar part of the interlocking H's. One false move and it would be ruined.

"Hey, how does it feel to be so talented?" Fletcher muttered over his sketch pad.

"Fletcher, dahling, we can't all be born *artistes*," Joss said, sending tiny chips of wood flying as she whittled away on her design.

"This is hopeless," Fletcher sighed a moment later, wiping his forehead with the back of his hand and smudging himself with charcoal. "This is supposed to be the pond with all those dumb lily pads. Only I swear it's looking more and more like a pepperoni pizza."

Joss bent closer over her woodcut, ignoring his remarks. She wanted to try and finish up today.

"Maybe you should start a new style of painting," Laura said to Fletcher. "It could be called Art Garbahge."

"I wouldn't talk. My four-year-old brother draws better than that," Fletcher snapped, pointing his piece of charcoal disdainfully at Laura's sketch pad.

Laura looked stung, and turned as pink as her outfit. She had only been joking. And Fletcher knew that. He was just being mean, but then, he didn't like Laura. He thought she was an airhead. "Her idea of heavy brainwork is to flip through a fashion magazine," he'd once said. Well, she was no intellectual giant, but Joss liked her anyway. Twenty-three pairs of shoes and all.

"Fletcher, why don't you try *fermez*-ing *votre bouche*," Joss said flatly. "I can't concentrate with you mouthing off, and if I don't watch out, I could sl—"

Slip. That's what Joss had been about to say when suddenly the small woodcutting knife seemed to take on a life of its own and sliced into the fleshy part of her left palm.

"Miss Kas-*per*," Joss whispered in panic. The knife was stuck in her hand. And there was blood. Lots of it.

Joss saw the horrified look on Laura Weiss' face. Her shocking pink blouse was spattered with red. Then it seemed as if lots of flashbulbs were popping all at once. The next thing Joss saw was the faces of Miss Kasper and her classmates, unnaturally large, looming above her.

"You're okay, Jocelyn," Miss Kasper kept assuring her in a calm voice.

Joss tried to focus on her hand. It throbbed terribly.

But the knife was gone, thank goodness. And a hand-kerchief was now tied tightly around her hand.

"Do you think you can walk?" asked Miss Kasper.

Joss blinked. She felt so stupid with everyone star-ing at her. "Sure I can," she croaked to Miss Kasper.

"My car is nearby. You just lean on me."

But Joss, who easily had five inches on frail little Miss Kasper, buckled. Twig took over. He grabbed Joss under her arm, steered her to the car, then slid in beside her.

A few minutes later Miss Kasper pulled to a stop at Higham Community Hospital.

"Where can we reach either of your parents?" a nurse in the emergency room asked. "We'll need someone's consent before a doctor can stitch you up."

"Stitches!" Joss yelped louder than she intended. "Wouldn't a large Band-Aid do?"

The nurse just stood there, pencil poised, waiting for the number.

Even though it was four thirty, Mom wasn't home. Then Joss remembered she had said she'd be at the old Historical Society building doing research on the houses on the tour. But whoever answered said Mom hadn't been there all day.

"Can you think of any other number she might be at?" the nurse asked with visible impatience. "Or where we might contact your father?"

Joss shook her head. Dad could be anywhere. At classes. At a faculty meeting. Miss Kasper promised to wait with her, but Twig had to make a quick exit.

"Uh, listen, I'd like to hang around, but my tutor's coming at five, and if I don't show up, well, I hate to think what my dad'll do." Twig waved as he went out the swinging doors of the emergency room. "I'll call you tonight to see how you're doing."

"Twig's got a good head on his shoulders," Miss Kasper said a moment later. "When you blacked out, he knew just what to do to stop the blood. . . . It's too bad he doesn't bother to apply himself more. He's basically a bright boy."

Joss nodded absently. She was thinking about what a scene she'd made. Blacking out. Talk about melodrama. But she had to admit it had given her a nice feeling to lean on Twig. And tonight! He had said he'd call. Of course he was probably only being polite.

Finally, *finally*, at quarter of six Mom answered the phone at home. Ten minutes later she was in the emergency room.

"Gee, Ma. Nice of you to show up," Joss said. "Where have you *been*?"

"Honey. Forgive me. *Please*. It's just been one of those days. A million and one errands. I feel horrible I wasn't home before. Horrible," Mom repeated, and her eyes started to well up with tears.

"Mom, Mom. It's okay. Take it easy," Joss said quickly, embarrassed. "It's not like you knew I was going to go and pull a cool move like this!"

Mom nodded distractedly. She thanked Miss Kasper for her help. Then it was time for Joss to go into the examination room, where a young doctor went to work on her hand.

Joss squeezed Mom's shoulder as she felt the sharp prick of the novocaine needle and then heard—which was worse—the steady snip-snip as the doctor sewed up her numb hand.

She concentrated hard on a small brass plaque over the door. "In memory of Anna Searles Lorimer," it said. Had to be one of Twig's relatives, Joss thought. The Lorimers donated scads of money to everything.

"Honey, you're really being brave. It'll be finished soon," Mom promised.

By six thirty they were in Mom's beat-up VW convertible, driving home.

"Is your hand hurting a lot, honey?" Mom inquired, her voice full of concern.

"Not too bad. It's still kind of numb."

"When we get home, you just take it easy. Stretch out on the sofa. Whatever you need, I'll get," her mother said, flashing a nervous smile. "You won't have to budge."

"*Ma*-a, will you quit acting like this was your fault," Joss said with irritation. "I'm all right. Honest."

"Okay, honey. Okay," Mom answered quickly, still looking upset.

They drove for a while in silence. For the first time Joss noticed her mother had on a good dress and her gold knot earrings.

"Hey, Mom! Are you wearing eye makeup?" asked Joss. "I don't believe it."

Mom blinked and reddened as if she'd forgotten about it. "Silly, huh?" Mom paused for a second. "I remember when I was about your age, I had this friend—Amy Wallenberg—and whenever we were feeling crummy, she and I would both go to Woolworth's and practically buy out the makeup department." Mom laughed. "When I think how many hours we spent trying to get our eyeliner on perfectly straight. And then we'd glop on pearlized blue shadow all the way up to our eyebrows—it was called the Cleopatra look!"

"Laura's always telling me how I should wear makeup. She says there's nothing wrong with helping nature along."

"Well, I love your face exactly the way it is."

"Oh, *Ma*," Joss said indulgently. "You have to say that. You're my mother. If I had no nose, you'd still say you loved my face just the way it was."

"Maybe so," Mom admitted, smiling, as she pulled over to the curb.

"Why are we stopping?"

"You stay here. I'm just going to pick up a few things at The Epicurean. I'll only be a minute."

Her mother must have blown a bundle, because she came out with a ton of shrimp salad, stuffed avocados, and raspberries—all Joss' favorites.

"I was planning on getting something special tonight anyway," Mom said, sounding defensive again. "We all deserve a nice, relaxed meal."

But the meal turned out to be anything but relaxed.

"Poor Ducks," Daddy said at dinner. "That's truly suffering for the sake of art!" He sounded cheerier tonight, but then he'd just downed two pretty stiff vodkas.

Joss giggled, a little nervously. "Yeah, it was real clever on my part."

"And neither one of us around," Daddy continued, "while the very life's blood ran from you!" There seemed to be an edge to his joking, and Mom looked uncomfortable again.

"It was no big deal, Daddy," Joss assured him, digging into the raspberries. "It's not like I was on the critical list or anything."

"Where were you, anyway?" Daddy had turned to Mom. There was definitely an accusatory note in his voice.

"Oh, I had errands to do. And then with the tour coming up, I had to do some research at the Historical Society. . . ." Mom looked like she didn't want to talk about it.

"The tour. So what else is new?" Daddy said.

Joss stared down at her dessert. Hadn't the person at the Historical Society said that Mom hadn't been there all day? Why would Mom lie? Then Joss reassured herself that of course, she wouldn't. The lady must not have seen Mom. Or else Mom actually meant that she was at one of the tour houses, not the Historical Society itself. In any case, Joss was not about to bring it up. Not now.

It was a blessed relief when the phone rang. Joss

jumped from the table to answer it, hoping that it was Twig.

"Um . . . Is Professor Longman there, please?" a pleasantly husky female voice asked.

"Yes, he is," Joss said, disappointed. "May I tell him who's calling?" Normally she never asked that; it seemed so nosy, but Joss had a sneaking suspicion who it was.

There was the slightest hesitation before the voice said, "Phoebe Jackson."

"Hold on one moment, please. Daddy, it's for you," Joss called out. "Phoebe Jackson."

"I'll take it in my office." Daddy was already hurrying from the dining room. Joss hung up once she heard the click on the other extension. A moment later there was a loud laugh, then silence, then more laughing.

Joss passed by the dining room. Mom was still there, drinking her coffee. When was the last time Daddy had laughed that way with Mom? Joss wondered. Was Mom wondering the same thing, too? Poor Mom. She looked small and forlorn sitting there. Joss paused by the archway entrance. The nice dress. The earrings. The makeup. Was Mom trying to make a special effort for Daddy's sake? That made Joss even sadder.

"Is it okay if I go upstairs?" Joss asked. "I have a ton of studying to do."

Mom nodded, and Joss left. She felt guilty for abandoning Mom, but she wanted to get away from both her parents. Gently touching the bandage on her

35

hand, she waggled her thumb to see how sore the cut was. It was an outright lie what she'd told Mom. About studying. She had no intention of opening a book. How could she when Twig might call any minute?

As she trudged up the stairs, Joss found herself thinking of Millicent Mortimer and the parts of her diary where she'd written about meeting her true love, Elliot Bender.

A moment later Joss was in the attic, switching on the light. Dusty, dark, and always stultifyingly hot, the attic was filled with Millicent's forgotten belongings. All the good stuff had been carted off long ago by the cousin in Boston who had inherited everything. She probably didn't even know the diary existed; Joss had discovered it herself, quite by accident, in the crack between two steamer trunks.

Sitting cross-legged on the floor, Joss leafed carefully through the diary. It went all the way from 1912, just before Millicent's twelfth birthday, to 1918 when her fiancé, Elliot Bender, was killed in World War I.

Joss stopped when she came to the entry for June 14, 1916, three days after Millie had met Elliot at a big party at the Lorimers'. Of all places.

"Dear diary," Millie had begun.

I cannot stand another minute of this waiting. Surely if Elliot Bender cared at all for me, I would have heard from him by now. Papa scolded me—

Here the entry broke off, and when it began again it was in a darker shade of ink.

Dear diary, I am sorry for leaving you so abruptly, but Clara and her beau Jack Lorimer came by with—yes! you have guessed it—Elliot Bender. What a wonderful day we had picnicking at Letchworth Park. Elliot has lent me a book of poems by Rupert Brooke, whom he greatly admires. I am going to read them this evening so when I see him next time (oh, I pray it is soon, dear diary!) I may speak to him with some intelligence.

Joss continued reading through the entries for the summer of 1916, which told of further excursions to Letchworth Park with Jack and Clara, outdoor "musicales" at the Higham band shell in the center of town, and long soul-searching conversations with Elliot held on the front porch, never far from her papa's watchful eye.

Then, before she closed the diary, Joss flipped to the very last page, which Millie had written right after she learned Elliot had been shot in France. All it said was "For me there will never be another." Joss' eyes started to burn and fill up every time she read that stark, hopeless sentence. It was so sad. And so romantic. Joss could imagine Millie's father and all her friends telling her that in time she would get over her grief for Elliot and find someone else. But she hadn't. She had remained faithful to his memory to her dying day. That was true love, all right. For keeps. Forever. Joss turned off the attic light and went down to her room. What was it like to fall in love? She'd asked Mom that question about a million times. "I can't describe it" was always her mother's standard, inadequate reply. "You'll find out for yourself one day. But I can tell you it's wonderful. And frightening, too—to care so much for somebody that you feel their very existence is what makes *you* alive, keeps *you* breathing."

What would have happened if Daddy had gone to Vietnam and been killed? Joss bet Mom never would have fallen in love with anybody else, either. Maybe she too would have turned into a lonely, eccentric old lady like Millie.

The phone jangled, bursting Joss' vision of an elderly Mom in farmer's overalls and cut-out sneakers. She pounced on the receiver, but it was only Laura, assuring Joss that she had already soaked the blood-stains out of her pink blouse. Later Miss Kasper called, and after that Fletcher checked in.

"So give me the gory details."

"I hate to disappoint you, Fletcher, but it wasn't very exciting. I got a few stitches is all."

"Thank God they managed to save the hand."

Joss laughed. "Yes. The miracles of modern medicine."

"Hey, everybody got a real kick seeing Twig play White Knight. . . . I bet you didn't mind it either. . . . 'Oh, Twig! My hero! Sigh, sigh!' " Fletcher chirped in a high voice. Then he switched to a low bass. " 'Uh, gee, Jocelyn. It was nothing.' " Fletcher started laughing.

"It's nice you get such a charge out of yourself, Fletcher. Listen, I've got to go."

"Oh, don't be so sensitive, Joss. I was only kidding."

"Okay," Joss said grudgingly. "But I really do have to go. I'm tired, and my hand still hurts."

"I guess I can relate to that."

Joss smiled to herself.

"See you tomorrow," they both said in unison.

After she hung up, Joss stared at the phone, willing it to ring. It remained maddeningly silent. Twig's not going to call, she told herself.

Locking the bathroom door behind her, Joss filled the giant tub with the funny claw feet and began the messy job of washing her hair one-handed under the faucet. Of course, she could call Mom for help, but lately she didn't want anyone to see her naked. It was as if her body had suddenly gone out of control. Inside she was the same old Joss, or almost, anyway, but on the outside there was a whole new wrapping. Somehow the two didn't go together at all.

Joss stared down at her breasts. Why couldn't she be built more like Mom? she thought. Thin and blessedly flat chested.

As she was rinsing her hair, Joss thought she heard her mother's muffled voice outside the door. Off went the faucet.

"It's Twig Lorimer," her mother was shouting. "Should I tell him you'll call back?"

"*No!* I'll be right there!"

Clutching a bath towel around her, Joss left a trail of wet footprints as she raced down the hall.

"Who've you been talking to all night?" said Twig in his familiar New England twang.

"Oh, some kids from school." Joss' voice sounded high-pitched and nervous to her, and her heart was thumping so loudly, it was a wonder Twig couldn't hear it, too. "Miss Kasper called a little while ago."

"She's nice," Twig observed.

"Yeah," Joss remarked. "She is."

"So, how's your hand?"

"Oh, okay, I guess."

"Well, that's good."

What to say now? "Yeah, I was lucky. The doctor told us if the knife had gone a little deeper, it would have cut into an artery, and then forget it. I would have been gushing blood all over the place." *Terrific. This was just what Twig wanted to hear. He was probably ready to throw up on the other end.*

"Well, I only called to see how you were," Twig said flatly.

Yeah, and now he was probably wishing he hadn't.

There was an awkward pause.

"Well, thanks, Twig. . . . 'Bye."

Click. Joss heard Twig hang up. Phone call *finito*.

Later that night, when she was trying to fall asleep, Joss played back their conversation over and over

40

again. Furious at herself, she thought of all the cool things that she should have said but hadn't. Still, Twig *had* called. That was something.

Careful not to hurt her bad hand, Joss plumped her pillow into a nice comfy shape and hugged it to her. She thought about Twig on one end of the phone and herself on the other, in nothing but a towel. What if Twig had been able to see her?

Joss decided maybe she wouldn't have minded. Oh, God! She loved him so much. She loved the veins in his arms that popped up like thin ropes running from his elbow to his wrist whenever he copied down homework assignments. She loved the way he said "really" instead of "yes" when he was agreeing with somebody. She loved how his voice hardly ever cracked, like the other boys'. Joss even loved the way he rolled up his shirt sleeves. Sometimes it seemed to her that she spent the entire school day spying on Twig. Did he know it?

Joss hugged the pillow tighter. She bet Twig had gone pretty far. He just looked like he had lots of experience; plus she'd heard he went out with older girls.

Closing her eyes, Joss pictured him lying on the bed beside her, trying to get her to—to get her to do what? Joss couldn't quite pin it down. Sex was such a big question mark. She tried to imagine what it would be like to kiss Twig. Hell! Who was she kidding? What would it be like to kiss anybody?

Wetting her lips, Joss puckered up and tried it with

her pillow. But all she got was the dry taste of one-hundred-percent cotton percale. If only it wasn't so hopeless, Joss thought as she burrowed under her quilt. If only there was a magic way to make Twig love her back!

Three

Joss rang Fletcher's doorbell and waited to be let in. Their French test was the day after tomorrow, and they'd decided to study for it together.

The shutter behind the peephole blinked open. Joss hoped it was not Fletcher's father on the other side. He made Joss nervous. He always seemed to be watching her every move, as if he was trying to determine the state of her mental health. Joss was quite sure the prognosis was not encouraging.

The door opened. Fletcher's mother. "Oh, Joss. It's YOU. I thought it might be ANOTHER patient," gushed Mrs. Dwoskin, who had a habit of speaking in capital letters. "It's almost EXAM time at the college, you know, and that's always the doctor's busiest season! It seems EVERYONE is on the verge of a nervous collapse. They've been coming here in DROVES! Well, don't stand there, dear. Come in, come in, come IN."

Joss came in.

"Fletcher's up in his room. If you two want anything, just YELL."

Joss murmured thanks as she climbed the stairs. Mrs. Dwoskin needn't have bothered informing Joss of Fletcher's whereabouts. When at home he seldom ventured outside his room, which was off limits to everybody, most especially Reginald, Fletcher's four-year-old brother.

As a baby Reginald had been pudgy-cute, but now he was just plain fat. Plus he seemed to have developed some type of inner radar—an uncanny sixth sense—for saying exactly what you didn't want to hear.

The last time Joss had been over, she'd almost died. Reginald had pointed boldly at her chest and lisped, "Joth hath big boobies."

"REG-I-NALD!" Mrs. Dwoskin had exclaimed in front of the entire family. "You KNOW we never use SILLY words like that. . . . We don't say BOOBIES. We say BREASTS."

Thank goodness Reginald was nowhere in sight tonight. Joss rapped on Fletcher's door, ignoring the sign that said, "Closed for Repairs."

"*C'est moi*," she called in.

"*Entrez.*"

As usual Fletcher's room was a mess. A dangerous mess. Tall, tipsy stacks of books and record albums threatened to crash down and clunk her on the head. Once, when she'd been barefoot, Joss had sliced her big toe on a stale hero sandwich underneath the bed.

She found Fletcher sitting powwow style on his unmade bed, surrounded by several shredded candy wrappers and a pile of old *Mad* magazines. He was staring intently at a heavy textbook that was propped against his pillow.

"C'mere, Joss," Fletcher said through a mouthful of chocolate. "I took this book from Dad's office. Wait'll you see these pictures."

Warily Joss plunked down her books on Fletcher's desk. The last time he had been deeply engrossed in one of his father's textbooks, it had turned out to be *The Illustrated Manual of Sex Therapy*. "Lookit, Fletcher. I came here to study. That was the only reason Ma let me out on a school night."

"Don't be such a poop. This'll only take a minute." Fletcher swiveled around so that his legs dropped to the floor, and spread open the book on his lap. As he did, Joss caught the title. *Mental Imagery and the Subconscious*. That sounded harmless enough, she supposed. She inched closer.

"Well, what do you see?" Fletcher was pointing to a picture of a lady at a dressing table looking into a mirror.

Joss shrugged. "A lady at a dressing table looking into a mirror."

45

"Right." Fletcher nodded slowly, pursing his lips together, the way his father often did. "And now what else do you see? Look closely, Jocelyn," he instructed patiently.

Blankly Joss stared at the page. "Nothing else. All I see is the lady." She began to grow annoyed. Who did Fletcher think he was, anyway? Some budding Sigmund Freud?

"Jocelyn! It's staring you right in the face. Look!" Fletcher's cool professional manner was slipping. "Can't you see that it's also a skull?"

"Wha-a-a?"

Impatiently Fletcher tapped his finger on the woman's head of dark hair and then on her reflected face in the mirror. "*See?* Here are the two empty eye sockets . . . and the top of the mirror, where it's rounded, is the top of the skull." Fletcher glanced at Joss to see if what he said was penetrating. "Look, dummy. And those ruffles on the dressing table are the mouth and teeth. . . ."

"Ooh! *Now* I see!"

Fletcher smacked the side of his head. "Finally. Finally."

Once Joss squinted her eyes so that the small details began to blur, and all she could make out was the picture as a whole, it did rearrange itself into a grinning death's-head. "That's creepy." She squinched up her nose. "What's it mean?"

"I don't know." Fletcher still sounded aggravated. "But you're supposed to see *both* things."

"Well, I like seeing just the lady better, anyway," Joss said defensively. She positioned herself at Fletcher's desk, cleared away some of the clutter, and spread out her pens and books.

Fletcher shut his book, annoyed. "That's so typical of you. See No Evil. Hear No Evil. Speak No Evil. . . . Remember your *Wonderful World of Nature* book?" When they'd been younger, Fletcher used to get practically apoplectic because Joss refused to look at the page with a huge hairy tarantula on it.

"Lookit, Fletcher. Are we here to psychoanalyze me or study French?"

"Oh, study French, I suppose," Fletcher conceded grouchily. He rummaged under the covers until he found his Larousse *grammaire*, and for the next hour they diligently drilled each other on irregular verbs.

"*Boire* . . . to drink. *Je bois* . . . I drink. *Tu bois* . . . you drink. *Il boit. Elle boit* . . ." Joss paused from her recitation and looked up to find Fletcher staring at her.

"Hey, what's so fascinating?"

"Nothing." Fletcher looked embarrassed now. "I was just noticing your hair. It's sort of the color of honey."

"It's filthy is what it is. If I don't wash it tonight, it's going to walk off and wash itself," she said self-consciously. It gave her the creeps to have Fletcher— well, *examining* her. They'd known each other for six years. Had he really just noticed what color hair she had?

Nervously Joss clasped her hands together and bent her fingers back, cracking her knuckles loudly.

"*Je déteste* irregular verbs," she said just to say something. "Plus all this stuff about *boire* is making me thirsty. I'm going to go get us some Cokes, okay?"

When she came back, Fletcher was stretched out on his bed, staring at the ceiling. He took one of the soda cans and rested it on his chest.

"What do you say we stop studying tonight? We've still got a while before the test . . . and you know my motto." Fletcher tried to make his voice go deep and growly. " 'Never put off until tomorrow what you can do the day after.' "

Joss made a weak face. Fletcher's imitation of W. C. Fields was practically indistinguishable from his imitation of Humphrey Bogart . . . or his imitation of Mae West. Joss wavered for a moment before shutting her notebook with a pleasing thud. "Okay, W. C., I feel like I have most of the stuff down anyway."

She began gathering up her books to go.

Fletcher sat up. "Wait, Joss. You don't have to leave yet. Stay and we can do something fun."

"Like what, for instance?"

"I don't know. . . . We could listen in on my father and his patient. If you hold a glass up to the kitchen wall, you can hear into his study pretty well."

"That's a truly cruddy idea, Fletcher." Joss thought of the sad, red-eyed girls, clutching crumpled wads of Kleenex, whom she sometimes saw emerging from

Dr. Dwoskin's office. She did not want to know their secret troubles.

"What about playing some trick phone calls?"

Joss shrugged. The idea really didn't grab her. "On who?" she asked.

"Mmm. I don't know." Fletcher looked like he was thinking hard. "How about Twig?"

Joss tried to remain expressionless. Last night when she'd been out baby-sitting, she'd done just that. Called Twig. The second she'd heard his voice, she'd hung up.

"I have a better idea," she said, hoping to divert Fletcher. "Let's call up a Bronwyn girl and you can pretend you're some guy from Cranhurst who wants a date."

"Awright! I like it! I like it!" Fletcher reached for the phone by his nightstand. "And I know just who to call. That girl who's got your dad for her advisor. The one that's such a knockout. You know who I mean."

Joss certainly did. Fletcher was talking about Phoebe Jackson. He'd seen her once at Joss' house. "Your father really has it rough," he'd said enviously. "Your mom better watch out with that kind of competition."

Joss had not appreciated that remark. Nor had she liked it when Fletcher reported back to her that he'd seen her father and Phoebe at the Bronwyn Student Union together.

"So? Is it a crime for him to have a cup of coffee

with one of his students?" Joss had tried to sound unconcerned. "They probably just ran into each other and decided to sit at the same table."

Fletcher snapped his fingers. "Phoebe . . . Phoebe Jackson! That's her name!"

"I'm not sure. I don't remember." But there was no stopping Fletcher. He was already calling Bronwyn College information for her number. A crazy thought flashed through Joss' mind. What if her father was with Phoebe Jackson this very second? Joss imagined him picking up the phone in Phoebe's room right now. Of course, that was totally insane. Out of the question. All the same, Joss felt her entire body tense when Fletcher asked, "Is Phoebe there?" and then relax as he turned to her, nodding excitedly and mouthing the words, "It's her."

"Uh, listen, Phoebe. You don't know me. But my name is Lance. Lance Todd."

Joss folded her arms and shook her head. Where on earth did Fletcher dream up these names?

"A friend of mine gave me your number," Fletcher went on, trying hard to sound old and sophisticated. Maybe he could have fooled Reginald, but Joss doubted it.

"You've probably seen me around campus," he continued. "People tell me I look a lot like Tom Selleck."

Tom Selleck! Joss nearly keeled over.

"My major? Why—uh—it's English." Pause. "You, too! Yeah, that is some coincidence. So what courses are you taking?" Another pause. "Professor Long-man's course on James Joyce. Oh yeah? What's it like? I hear the guy's kind of a moron." Joss clobbered Fletcher on the shoulder and swatted at the receiver so she could listen in, but Fletcher elbowed her out of the way and cradled the phone closer to him.

"Oh? Is that so?" Fletcher said.

"Come on, Fletcher. What's she saying?" Joss made another swipe at the phone. Suddenly she felt scared. "Fletcher, this is dumb. Hang up now." What if some-how Daddy found out they were calling up his stu-dents? Joss tugged at Fletcher's arm. "Get off. She's going to know this is a put-on."

"Pardon me, Phoebe. Could you hold on for one minute? I think one of my fraternity brothers is calling me." Fletcher cupped his hand over the receiver. "Will you kindly shut up? You're gonna wreck every-thing."

"This is nuts!" Joss hissed. That was the trouble with Fletcher. He got so carried away with things.

"Sorry for the interruption." Fletcher was back on the phone with his fake college voice. "Oh? Why do you have to get off so fast?" There was another pause. A longer one. "Well, I'm sorry to hear that." And then he hung up.

"Well, thanks a lot, Jocelyn," Fletcher said in his regular voice. "You had to go and blow it for me."

Joss shook her head in disbelief. "Give me a break, Fletcher. You really think you could've had a date

51

with her? What would you have done? Gotten Tom Selleck to stand in for you?"

"Of course not. But it was fun talking to her, and maybe she would have stayed on longer if she hadn't heard *you* in the background."

"Why? What'd she say?"

"If you must know"—Fletcher looked really ticked off now—"she said she was already kind of involved with someone and that, anyway, she liked older guys. Quote. Unquote. Satisfied?"

No, Joss was not. That definitely was *not* what she wanted to hear. Perhaps Phoebe had guessed the call was only a joke and was letting Fletcher know that she realized he was just a kid. Or did she honestly mean it about liking older guys? And if so, exactly how old? As old as her father?

"So? What did she have to say about Dad?" said Joss, trying not to seem overinterested.

"Never mind." Fletcher picked up his French book and pretended to study again.

"What!" Joss wanted to throttle Fletcher. She hated when he got his way.

"You yourself said it was a dumb thing to do." Fletcher's voice was infuriatingly reasonable. "So why bother discussing it?"

Joss just stood there, in the middle of his room, with her hands on her hips.

"Fletcher, you can be such an incredible creep sometimes."

"Listen, Jocelyn. I don't need to sit here and take abuse from you in my own house."

"Fine. Then I'll leave."

"Fine. Nobody's stopping you."

In one motion Joss swept up her books, flung them into her book bag, and clattered downstairs, nearly tripping in her clogs.

"And don't call me later, either," Fletcher shouted after her.

"Don't worry. I won't," Joss yelled back over her shoulder, even though she was always the one who ended up restoring peace between them.

As she reached the front door, Reginald suddenly popped out from behind a large potted palm. He was dressed in full cowboy regalia and brandished a large water pistol.

"Got you, you dirty varmint," he crowed triumphantly. "Right in the boobies!"

Water dripping down the front of her shirt, Joss sputtered something incomprehensible before she slammed the door behind her.

Four

"I could kill Madame Fein. Leave it to that old witch to stick in stuff she never even went over in class. My average is going to be wrecked," wailed Bobo.

They were ringed around the large back table at Phil's Pizza Parlor—Bobo, Twig, Michelle, Fletcher, Laura, and Joss—commiserating over the French test, which *had* been a killer.

Joss had blown two whole conjugations. She'd just checked them out in her grammar book. But that was not the only reason for her rotten mood. She cast a sideways glance at Fletcher, whose face was practically buried in a slice of Phil's finest. Their fight from the night before last still had her mad. . . . No, that was not quite true, Joss admitted to herself as she licked

54

the sticky rim of her pleated cup of Italian ice. What really made her so angry was that, as always, she had knuckled under and apologized. All yesterday Fletcher had refused to speak to her, so today, right before the test, Joss had ambled over to his desk and said, "Listen, Fletcher, I'm sorry if I acted dumb the other night. Let's just forget about it, okay?"

"Welllllll . . . all right," Fletcher had conceded magnanimously. But it wasn't all right. Why was she such a spineless jellyfish? Such a wimp?

"I know what. I'll throw a party. That should cheer me up," Bobo suddenly announced. "Besides, it's about time *someone* in this poky town had a party. It's pathetic." Bobo pulled a face, pouting perfect lips.

"Hear, hear," Fletcher said as he continued to work his way through the pizza.

"I'll help you plan for the party. Whatever you want I could do," Michelle volunteered eagerly. She had been the hostess of this year's only girl-boy party. All night the boys had stayed huddled together at one end of the Klines' living room, cracking dumb jokes and punching each other in the arm, while the girls sat around demurely, trying hard to look as if they were having fun. Twig had not even been there; he'd come down with the flu.

"Remember that guacamole dip I had at my party, Bobo?" Michelle went on excitedly. "You said how you liked it so much. Well, I could get my mom to make some for your party, too."

"Mmmmm. That's sweet, Michelle. We'll see." Bobo bestowed a brief, regal smile on her loyal subject. "What I really need is somebody to set up my stereo down in the basement." Bobo turned to Twig, sitting to her right, and pressed him lightly on the arm. "Twig, do you think you could do it for me?" Bobo bit her lower lip and waited.

"No problem," said Twig, who was leaning back on two legs of his chair, balanced precariously against the wall. "If you ask me nicely, I might even donate my record collection for the occasion."

Joss felt sick. Clever, wily, tricky Bobo had managed to lure Twig over to her house. Alone! Joss had known Twig would say yes. Was he just being nice? Or did he like Bobo? It was so hard to tell about Twig.

Take this morning in Natural Sciences. Mr. Heinz had had them dissecting horrid, dead, brown flatworms, and Joss' bandaged hand made the job doubly difficult.

"Allow me," Twig had offered, brandishing his tiny knife like a knight with raised sword, and he'd spent the rest of the period patiently helping Joss do the dirty work. For a few moments Joss began to think that perhaps Twig might like her a little, but now she just didn't know.

"Oh, Twig! If you could lend me your records—especially whatever new stuff you have—that would be super. Absolutely super." Bobo was beaming now, and again she squeezed Twig's arm.

Joss flashed a murderous glare her way. She hated Bobo for touching Twig; for being *able* to touch him and act like it was no big deal.

Daintily Bobo sucked up the last of her diet soda. "Well, gotta go." She rose to her feet. "I told Mummy I'd pick Mignon up at the vet's. She got an infected paw, poor pooch."

Joss almost gagged. Why did Bobo think the tiniest, most boring details of her life were of supreme importance to everyone else?

Bobo's departure seemed to signal the breakup of the group. Michelle immediately went tagging after her, calling out for Bobo to wait up so she could walk with her. Then Twig left for his after-school tutoring, and a minute later Fletcher polished off the remains of his pizza crust and got up.

"You're going, too?" Laura asked Fletcher. She sounded disappointed.

"Yes. Try to be brave about it, sweetheart," Fletcher said in his Humphrey Bogart voice. "It's better for both of us this way. . . . Besides," Fletcher suddenly reverted to his normal voice, "I have to be at the orthodontist's at four o'clock."

Laura looked blankly at Fletcher.

"In case you're wondering, that was supposed to be Humphrey Bogart," Joss informed her.

"Oh!" Laura giggled. "Well . . . bye-bye, Bogey," she called as Fletcher departed. "He's so funny," she said to Joss a moment later. "He just cracks me up."

"Yes. Fletcher's a regular laugh riot," Joss responded sourly. Absently she crumpled up her paper cup and stared at Bobo's empty seat. She couldn't help wishing she was more above it all like Bobo. Bobo didn't seem to care much about anybody . . . except Twig, of course. It was obvious that Bobo had a gargantuan crush on him. In class she was always passing notes to him, and twice in folk dancing Bobo had actually had the guts to ask Twig to be her partner.

"Earth to Joss." Laura was waving her hands in front of her, trying to catch Joss' attention. "I said, do you have to go too, or can you stay for a little while?"

"No. Sure I can stay. I'm getting my stitches out today. Daddy's taking me over to the hospital. I'm supposed to meet him at his office, but I don't have to be there until quarter of five."

"Isn't it exciting about the party?" said Laura, who was a vision in yellow today—yellow knee socks, shorts, and button-down-collar shirt. Even yellow barrettes.

"Mmmm. I guess." The prospect of watching Twig and Bobo together all night was not exactly Joss' idea of a fun time. She could just picture them now, laughing, choosing what records to play, dancing in a dark corner to some slow song. . . . Joss heaved a weighty sigh.

"What's the matter, Joss?"

"Oh, I don't know. I just feel kind of blah. Maybe some more strawberry ice will pick me up," she said, feeling extremely virtuous because she had managed to stay away from the pizza.

Joss went over to the counter and stood, staring at a five-dollar bill taped above the cash register while one of the boys who made the pizzas scooped out another messy dollop of melting strawberry ice for her. Phil's was not what you'd call loaded with atmosphere. It was one of the few places in Higham that wasn't quaint or charming. The flesh-colored linoleum floor was scarred and cracked; the booths, upholstered in fake red leather, were patched with adhesive everywhere; and the scuffed walls were bare except for a couple of yellowed, curling travel posters of Italy that said, "Fly PAN AM."

Joss returned to the table, where Laura was busy flipping through *Seventeen.* She always seemed to have a stack of magazines with her, no matter where she went.

"I'm looking for a new hairstyle," Laura explained as she scanned the glossy pages. "I want to look really good for Bobo's party. It'll be the first party I've been to since I moved here." Laura paused. "Hmm. Here's one that it says is flattering if you have a prominent nose."

Laura wasn't bad-looking. She was short and petite with a pretty dimpled smile, and she was always perfectly groomed. But she had a real schnoz. There was really no other way to describe it, although Laura often referred to her nose as "aquiline." Her father had promised she could have a nose job as soon as she turned fifteen, and Laura was counting the days.

"I don't even want to go to Bobo's dumb party," Joss said without thinking.

"Oh, you're just saying that because you're scared she'll see to it that Twig is with her the whole time."

Joss fixed her eyes on a photograph in the magazine of a revoltingly beautiful model running along the ocean, an Irish setter chasing after her. "It's that obvious, huh? That I like Twig, I mean."

"Probably not to everyone. But I could tell." Laura smiled. "Don't worry, though. My lips are sealed."

Joss smiled back. Fletcher was wrong. Maybe Laura wasn't book smart, but she sure picked up on people.

"Why is it such a deep dark secret anyway?" Laura asked.

"I don't know. I guess it's that it's so hopeless." Joss slurped up some more ice, dripping a little onto Laura's magazine. "I feel stupid liking him so much. Boys who look like Twig just naturally belong with girls who look like Bobo . . . even their names go together."

"Honestly, Joss. You're not exactly Quasimondo yourself."

"I think you mean Quasi*modo*," Joss corrected.

"Whatever." Laura waved her hand impatiently. "You know what I mean. . . . You've got great hair. And your eyes are terrific. They look just like Sophia's."

"Sophia who?"

"*Loren*, dummy," said Laura, who was strictly on

a first-name basis with all celebrities. "You know, you should read more of these magazines. They all say the same stuff. If you feel good about yourself, then you send out a positive image. . . . Look at me. Some people might say my nose is ugly. But I like to think it makes me look interesting. Like Barbra's. A big nose didn't stop her from becoming a movie star."

"Then why are you going to have your nose fixed?"

"Because then I'll be an absolute knockout, and that'll be even better."

"Oh, Laura!" Joss laughed, although Laura did not seem to see any holes in her logic.

"Listen, you can't be such a dog or a certain some-one wouldn't have a crush on you," Laura continued.

"But Twig doesn't like me," Joss protested. "He may think I'm a nice kid, but that's all."

"Who said I was talking about Twig?" Laura answered mysteriously.

"Then who *are* you talking about?"

"Here. Take a look at this." Laura picked up another one of her magazines and was thumbing through it. "I was reading this in Study Hall." Laura passed Joss the magazine. At the top of the page she was pointing to, it said "Face Up to It," and below were lots of letters signed either "Desperate" or "Miserable" or just plain "Anonymous."

"Read the one at the bottom," Laura instructed.

I have been friends (strictly platonic) with this boy in my class for a long time. Now all of a sudden I am starting to like him, really like him, which

61

is too bad for me because as far as he's concerned, I'm still just his good buddy. The trouble is I don't want that anymore. My feelings have changed. Isn't there anything I can do to get him to notice I'm a girl?

The letter was signed "All or Nothing." Joss turned the page to see what advice there was.

"Don't bother with the answer," Laura said. "It's dumb. About how 'All or Nothing' should try acting more feminine." Laura folded her arms and looked at Joss expectantly. "Well?"

"Well, what?"

"Doesn't it remind you of somebody we know?" Joss shrugged. "No, not really."

"Jocelyn! Don't be dense," said Laura. "Fletcher could've written that exact same letter if you switch the girl and boy stuff around."

"Fletcher! What are you talking about!"

"Come on, Joss. You mean to tell me you haven't noticed he likes you?"

"That is absolutely the craziest thing I ever heard," Joss said loudly. A couple of kids at tables nearby turned their heads. Joss lowered her voice. "That's nuts," she reiterated softly.

"No, it isn't," Laura insisted. "I see the way he sometimes looks at you. Maybe *you* don't want to see it, but—"

"No, Laura. That's not it." Joss shook her head emphatically. "You happen to be way off base. I've known Fletcher for six years, and believe me, the idea of anything romantic between us is absurd."

"Suit yourself," said Laura in a voice that plainly said she knew better.

Later, as Joss walked across the Bronwyn campus on her way to meet Daddy, she reassured herself once again that Laura was out of her mind. She and Fletcher were just good friends. Period. Like they had always been. Like they would always be. That wouldn't ever change. . . . She simply wouldn't let it.

When she reached Bixby Hall, it took a moment for Joss to adjust her eyes to the shadowy dimness inside. The building seemed deserted, and, as Joss climbed the stone stairs to the second floor, her steps echoed so loudly that twice she turned to see if anyone was following her. She hurried down the long corridor. From the other end came the sound of laughter, Daddy's and someone else's.

"Friend or foe? Declare yourself," Daddy said after Joss knocked tentatively on his door.

Joss didn't know what to say. There was more laughing inside.

"Friend," Joss finally said. "It's me, Daddy," And she went inside.

"Oh, hello, Ducks!" said Daddy. He was sitting at his desk with his feet propped up. Across from him was Phoebe Jackson. She was standing, but it looked like she had gotten up that very instant. All Joss could think about was the phone call she and Fletcher had made the other night, and she felt herself redden.

"Sorry. Didn't mean to barge in," she mumbled.

"No problem." Daddy smiled. He looked more re-laxed than Joss had seen him in ages. "You remember Phoebe Jackson, don't you?"

Remember her? Was it likely you'd forget someone who could win a Brooke Shields look-alike contest? Joss acknowledged Phoebe with a jerky nod.

Phoebe smiled. She was wearing jeans and a turtle-neck. Her long hair was braided down her back. She looked gorgeous. Capital G.

"Your father was just telling me about the Monty Python movie that was at the Buster Keaton last week. I missed it," Phoebe said in that pleasantly husky voice of hers.

"I dragged Joss to it," Daddy said. "I'm a horrible parent. I always take her to movies on school nights—providing they're ones *I* want to see!"

Joss just nodded and stood around like a lunk. She and Daddy had gone together while Mom stayed home studying. That had ticked Daddy off even though he had kept quiet about it.

"I think those guys are hysterical," Phoebe went on. "I mean, some of what they do is *so* gross, but they're so funny."

"I think they're dumb." That wasn't true, but Joss said it anyway.

Phoebe began to look uncomfortable. She cleared her throat. "Well, too bad I didn't know you needed company that night," she said to Daddy.

Just what was that crack supposed to mean? Joss scowled and didn't answer. She noticed Phoebe was clutching a pack of Pall Malls, the same brand of cigarettes her father smoked. That small connection rankled her, although she could not have said why.

"I suppose I should be heading over to Westcott Hall," Phoebe said. "I've got that ridiculous Biblical Imagery seminar at five thirty."

"The Gospel according to Malcolm Thornridge. Don't get me started on *him*," Daddy said. They both laughed again.

Once she was at the door, Phoebe turned. "Nice to see you, Joss. . . . Catch you later," she said to Daddy with a wave. Then she left, her long braid twitching back and forth behind her.

Catch you later. Joss did not like the sound of those words, and she remained stonily silent as Daddy gathered his papers and books into his old maroon book bag and locked the office door behind him. He was whistling, actually whistling, now.

Joss followed after him, her father's high spirits weighing heavily upon her. She began wondering exactly how often Phoebe Jackson dropped by Daddy's office and how long she stayed. Fletcher had spotted them together that one time in the Student Union. Were there other times? At other places?

In the car, Daddy continued to whistle and Joss to mope. At one point Joss nearly asked him if he'd heard anything more about his chances for tenure just to wreck his good mood, but she didn't. Instead she began counting traffic lights. If there turned out to be an even number by the time they reached the hospital, that meant her fears about Daddy and Phoebe were idiotic, groundless. But if there were an odd number of lights . . . well, then maybe she'd better really start worrying!

"You're not nervous about having the stitches out, are you?" Daddy patted Joss' shoulder with his free hand.

Joss frowned and shook her head. They zipped through the first traffic light just before it turned red.

"Something else bothering you, then?"

"No!" What was this? The Inquisition?

"Okay, okay. I'll back off." Daddy concentrated on the road. Another traffic light passed by. That made two. "When I think of all the things you could have inherited from me—my razor wit, my indefatigable charm—and you had to go and pick my rotten disposition."

Slumped against the car seat, Joss managed a half-hearted laugh. Sometimes it really did seem as if she was a mixture of the worst parts of both her parents. Moody and always worrying about everything like Daddy without any of his outgoing nature. No, in that respect she was much more like Mom. Shy and self-conscious.

"Believe me. I was much worse at your age," Daddy confessed. "I perfected what I liked to think of as the Ultimate Sneer. Watch me. I can still do it." Daddy kept his eyes on the road while he curled his lower lip into a ridiculous leer. "See? Really has you intimidated, huh?"

"Oh, Daddy!" Joss couldn't help laughing. "Do you go on this way in class? I bet you do. I bet that's why all those girls are so crazy about you."

"They're not *all* crazy about me," her father disclaimed. "There are probably still one or two who haven't succumbed to my raw animal appeal."

"That girl Phoebe sure seems to like you a lot." Joss felt her heart start to pound. She couldn't believe she'd actually come out and said that.

"Joss, don't be an imbecile," Daddy said with sudden brusqueness. "We're just friends. She's my student. I'm practically old enough to be her father, to coin a phrase."

That doesn't matter, Joss felt like blurting out. She goes for older guys.

"Here we are," Daddy stated, cutting the conversation short. They stopped at the traffic light by the intersection to the hospital. The *third* traffic light.

Five

Rats! Where was her denim skirt? Joss rummaged around the inside of her closet, pushing aside hanger after hanger.

It was Thursday, the night of the lecture, and she was alone in the house. Her mother had already been dashing out when she came home from school.

"Look nice tonight, honey. No jeans, okay?" were her parting words.

Dismally Joss surveyed the contents of her closet. Her red shirtwaist, the one halfway decent dress she owned, was now much too short and so tight across the chest that she could barely close the buttons. God! At this rate she'd be wearing a 48Z bra by the time she turned fourteen.

At last the skirt turned up. Oh well. It didn't look *too* wrinkled.

Joss was breathing in deeply to zip up the zipper when the phone rang.

It was her father calling from his office.

"Listen, Ducks. You go on and eat without me. I've got a hell of a backlog of papers to grade." Her father's voice sounded slightly muffled, as if his hand was cupped over the receiver. "I'll pick you up at seven fifteen. . . . Then we can both go and hear the *illustrious* Professor Macdunna."

"Just remember Ma wants us there by seven thirty."

Joss stared at the receiver after she hung up, feeling uneasy. Was it her imagination or had she heard someone laughing in the background?

Joss retrieved her clogs from under her bed, slipped into them, and sniffed a couple of times under the arms of the shirt she was wearing. It was a pale pink oxford button-down, and in school today Twig had told her he liked it. Twig. He was almost certain to be there tonight. He'd mentioned something about it during lunch.

Odds were Fletcher would put in an appearance too, seeing that there was free food after.

Down deep Joss was half hoping Fletcher wouldn't show up. With Fletcher around, if she so much as uttered one word to Twig, she'd never hear the end of it. Joss ran a comb through her hair. Funny. In all the years they'd been friends, it had never mattered that Fletcher was a boy. Yet now, more and more, Joss felt she had to keep secrets from him. Well, at least there was Laura to confide in.

"Yup, you've sure got it bad," Laura had said with a sympathetic nod after lunch today. Twig had been sitting at the next table, and when he got up, Laura caught Joss stuffing his crumpled-up paper napkin into her purse. For a memento.

Joss was mortified. This was how girls acted in dopey romance novels. Laura, however, saw nothing strange about her behavior.

"Listen, I was the exact same way about this boy in California," Laura said. "I was *crazy* about him. I used to swipe his cigarette butts. By the time I moved, I had a whole collection!"

Joss glanced at the clock. Oh, no. It was later than she'd thought. She'd have to skip dinner. There was just time to run a comb through her hair and give herself one last once-over before waiting outside for Daddy.

But it was almost seven thirty before Daddy finally pulled up in front of the house. Joss, growing angrier by the second, was pacing back and forth on the sidewalk when she saw Daddy come tooling down the street.

The car horn tooted, three shorts and a long. Her father's customary way of announcing his arrival.

"Hop in, Ducks." Her father leaned over to open the door.

"Daddy! Ma's going to kill us."

"Sorry I'm late," Daddy said, not looking sorry at all. "Just lost track of time, I guess."

Sure. Sure. Joss slid into the passenger seat beside him. Dr. Dwoskin claimed that people who were late simply didn't want to get where they were going.

"Ready for the big night?" Daddy asked. "I don't know about you, Ducks, but I for one am just swelling with civic pride."

"Daddy, don't be that way." Joss wondered if her father had had a drink before driving over to get her. His eyes looked heavy lidded and a little bloodshot, but maybe he was just tired. Joss chewed on her lower lip. If he had stopped somewhere for a drink, had he gone alone? Or had Phoebe— Joss stopped herself. She *had* to cut this stuff out. She was acting like a crazy jealous wife, for God's sake. If anybody was supposed to be doing the worrying, it was Mom.

"I think it'll be neat to hear all about our house. It's sort of like we're celebrities," Joss loyally asserted, although she really wasn't all that fired up about the lecture either.

A few minutes later they parked in a lot reserved for Bronwyn faculty and hurried down a street that curled around several of the main buildings on campus. Mom stood at the front entrance of a red brick building topped with an imposing white dome, Comstock Auditorium. She was flanked by several blue-haired ladies from the Historical Society who were helping pass out tour brochures. When she saw Daddy, she came running down the steps.

"Where have you been? Do you know what time it is? We're almost ready to start. I was beginning to think you weren't coming at all." Mom sounded angry and flustered. Her skin was flushed and blotchy.

"Sorry. Unavoidably detained" was all Daddy said.

For a miserable moment her mother and father stood there, staring at each other, neither one making a move. It wouldn't have killed Daddy to kiss Mom, Joss thought. Or just wish her luck. But he didn't.

"Don't worry, Mom, you'll do fine. Especially now that your cheering section has arrived." Joss made a stupid rah-rah gesture with her arms, and her mother squeezed her good hand.

"See you later, sweetie. After the lecture," she said without looking at Daddy, then pressed two brochures from her massive pile into Joss' hand.

The auditorium was more than half full. A respectable showing, Joss was relieved to see, as she and Daddy sank into two red plush seats near the back. Her father took off his jacket, and since Fletcher had made her promise to save him a seat, Joss draped the jacket over the armrest next to hers. Then she opened her brochure with the letterhead she'd designed. There was a small nick in the middle H from her fateful slip, but she didn't think someone who wasn't looking for it would notice. Actually it looked pretty professional, if she did say so herself.

"Okay if I sit here?" said someone.

Joss was about to say, "Sorry, it's saved," when she looked up and saw the voice belonged to Twig.

She gulped, a goofy-looking grin plastering itself across her face, and before there was time to decide what to answer, Twig was already squeezing into their row.

"How's it going?" he said to her, and then smiled tentatively at Joss' father.

Oh, yes. Yes. Introductions. She couldn't act like a complete cretin. "Um, Daddy. Uh, thith is Twig Lorimer." Thith? Swell! Now she was developing a speech impediment!

"Is your house on the tour, too?" Twig asked.

All Joss could manage was a smile and a nod.

"Are you going to stay for the party later?"

Another smile and nod. Oh God! Joss panicked inwardly. What was wrong with her? Why was it that she always acted like the village idiot around Twig? She could think of nothing—*rien, nada, niente*—to say.

Mercifully the auditorium began to darken. Then just before the lights went out altogether, Joss spotted Fletcher, peering nearsightedly down one row after another. She cupped a hand over her eyes and lowered her head.

"Hey, look. There's Fletcher." Twig started motioning to him. "Pssst, Fletcher. Over here."

Joss slunk down in her seat. Too late. She was positive Fletcher saw them. How could he miss? He was standing only a few feet away now. But suddenly his face grew stony; he looked off in the opposite direction, walked down to the front, and disappeared into a row on the other side of the aisle. Terrific! This

73

was exactly the kind of thing that Fletcher loved to blow up into an international incident.

There were a few raspy coughs from the audience now, and the sounds of people settling in their seats. Then Mom came out from the right of the stage and stood behind an oak lectern. She looked terrified—like she might puke or something—and for an instant Joss understood how parents must feel at their children's first school plays.

An earsplitting buzz from the microphone made Mom jump, but then in a surprisingly calm voice she welcomed everyone to the lecture, thanked the college for the use of the auditorium, and then went on to enumerate all of Professor Macdunna's many impressive accomplishments before she brought out a ruddy-faced, short, gray-haired man.

"Years and years ago, before I ever came to the United States," Professor Macdunna began in his clipped British accent, "when I tried to picture what a New England village would look like, I imagined a place remarkably like Higham."

One by one, slides of local landmarks flashed before the audience. The photos were really knockouts, a million times better than any of the corny postcards sold in the souvenir shops downtown. And Professor Macdunna turned out to be not so boring. Here Joss had lived in Higham six whole years, and not until tonight had she known that during Prohibition the basement of the Stiles Inn had been a thriving speak-easy! Bathtub gin and all.

Once or twice Joss glanced over to see if her father was at all impressed. But Daddy didn't even seem to be listening. His arms were folded across his chest, and he was staring off to the right of the auditorium stage, where Mom was still partially visible, standing in the wing, raptly focused on every word out of the professor's mouth.

"Oh, no," Twig suddenly whispered, covering his eyes as a shot of the front of his house was followed by a succession of slides showing rooms full of dark, uncomfortable-looking furniture, portraits of somber-looking ancestors peering down from the walls, and mammoth crystal chandeliers.

"And those are just the servants' quarters," Twig joked, but Joss thought he seemed genuinely embar-rassed.

Then suddenly, Joss' own house was on view—the dark-brown shingling, the white trim that badly needed a new coat of paint—and she sat up straighter in her seat to get a better look.

"Now we come to the last house on Sunday's tour. The Mortimer house on Willow Street. A house that, frankly, has added more to the lore of your town than to its aesthetics," said the professor before he launched into an account of old Mayor Stillwell's un-timely end, choking on a wishbone at Phineas Morti-mer's table.

"As for the structure itself, what we have, I'm afraid, is a rather excruciating if somewhat endearing exam-ple of Victorian excess."

"This guy doesn't like alliteration much, does he?" muttered Daddy, who was now paying attention.

Joss herself was a little puzzled by the professor's words. What did he mean, *excruciating*?

"While large by today's standards," he went on, "this house was actually quite modest in size for its time. Yet the original owner, the affluent merchant Phineas Mortimer, was bent on the *illusion* of grandeur. You'll notice, for example, that—"

A new slide focused in on the front of the house.

"—the deep Italianate porch is way out of proportion to the rest of the house. The effect is rather like a very small woman wearing a very large fancy hat. . . ."

Suddenly Joss remembered how she had bragged to Miss Kasper that their house was kitsch. Evidently that had *not* been a compliment. Here she'd always thought their house was weird but basically sort of elegant in a funky, faded way. Now it turned out it was just plain bad taste.

A moment later the lights brightened. While the crowd clapped enthusiastically, Daddy was already out of his seat and heading for the aisle.

"Wait up, Daddy. Where are you going? Aren't we staying for the party?" Joss asked.

Her father turned. "I don't know about you, but I'm going home. I've got an eight-o'clock class tomorrow and I'm shot."

"Daddy, no! Please!" Joss tried to keep her voice

76

calm. No scenes with Twig right here. "I'll come home with Ma later," she said, feeling for some reason like a traitor for even mentioning her mother.

Daddy looked tired. He shrugged again. "It's up to you."

Before there was time for Joss to try to change his mind, her father had disappeared into the crowd.

Twig cleared his throat. "Er—want to hit the party now?" he asked. "I'm starved. And the decent stuff always goes fast at these things."

Joss nodded. They went downstairs through the basement of the auditorium, following the signs and arrows that led to the lounge.

"Well, here we are!" Joss announced brightly at the entrance, and then slammed into Twig full force as they both went for the door at the same time.

Rubbing his forehead, Twig gave Joss a weak smile. "After you," he said warily and motioned her inside.

The party was already under way. Candlelight gave the room a soft, romantic glow, and the pleasant sound of people laughing mixed with the *chink-chink* of wine glasses. Everywhere Joss looked there were trays of food. Pearly pink shrimp. Tiny hot dogs wrapped in doughy blankets. Cheese cubes impaled on brightly colored, bewigged toothpicks. Joss' stomach lurched. She'd skipped dinner tonight, but no way was she going to pig out in front of Twig.

Twig helped himself to a hot dog, then speared a couple more with a toothpick.

"That's my sister over there." Twig pointed with the toothpick to a flock of girls by a fireplace.

"Oh, yeah?" Joss' stomach suddenly voiced a loud complaint. She pretended to cough and went into her smiling routine again. No need to worry about talking to Twig. Her stomach would do just fine without her.

"She's here with her roommates. They're all sophomores at Bronwyn."

"You're kidding! My mother goes there, too! She's a senior now. She dropped out of school a long time ago, so now she's finishing her degree." Joss had the feeling she was talking too loudly, but how else was she supposed to drown out the revolting gurgling going on inside her? "Um, does your sister like Bronwyn?"

Twig had started in on a bowl of shrimp now. "She hates it," he said. "But my parents made her go. All the girls in our family go to Bronwyn. It's a tradition. I had one cousin who went to Wellesley instead, and her mother didn't talk to her for months."

Joss laughed. Her hand wandered toward the shrimp, and one was in her mouth before she knew it. Her stomach murmured grateful thanks. "I think I want to go to Barnard. That's where my mother first went to college." She paused between bites of shrimp. "I guess it's unbelievably nerdy, me *wanting* to go to the same college as my mother. But I think it'd be neat to go to school in New York."

"I don't want to go to college, period. But at the

78

rate I'm going, I won't have to worry. I'll be lucky if I make it to ninth grade."

"You really hate school, huh?"

"Oh, I don't know." Twig cracked his knuckles reflectively. "Sometimes I try to figure out exactly when it was I first got stuck with this reputation for being such a goof-off. But all I know is now I feel like I have to live up to it."

"Are you going to be staying in Higham next year?" The very thought of Twig someplace else made Joss' heart twist up inside her.

"Nah. They're sending me off to a place in New Hampshire. You never heard of it, believe me. I think my father had to promise to pay for a whole new gym before they'd take me."

"Oh."

"Listen, I don't mean to sound so snotty," he said. "My parents really aren't bad. It's just that they got spoiled by my brother, who's a first-year law student at Harvard. And my sister, too—she's a cinch to make Phi Beta Kappa next year. I keep pointing out to my father that every generation of Lorimers has one black sheep. I'm actually just carrying on a family tradition." Twig smiled. With a smile like that, Joss figured he could rob banks and get away with it.

"What you said before. About being stuck with a reputation. I know what you mean." Joss relaxed a little more and helped herself to more shrimp. "It's the same with me. Only the opposite. For as long as I can remember, I've always been responsible and hardworking and cooperative. You know the type I'm talking about . . . the girl most likely to be chosen blackboard monitor.''

Twig laughed.

"Sure, go ahead and laugh if you want. But it gets to be a real drag. . . . Once when Fletcher and me were eight or nine he got me to steal some penny candy from Sweet Temptations. It was a dare. He didn't believe I'd actually go through with it. I mean, it was hardly the crime of the century, but I was so scared I practically went into cardiac arrest, and afterward I was so guilty I threw up all the candy.'' Joss couldn't believe she was telling Twig this stupid, gross story. She was positive none of Laura's magazines counseled discussing puking with the boy you wanted to win over, but Twig actually seemed interested.

"I think underneath I must be a very repressed person,'' Joss added, lowering her eyes pensively. Actually it was Fletcher who was always telling her that. He meant it as a put-down, of course, saying it simply to needle Joss or to goad her into doing things *he* wanted to do. But Joss sort of liked the idea of being repressed. It sounded a whole lot deeper and more mysterious than being just plain chicken.

"Yeah. I think I may be repressed, too,'' Twig said. Joss didn't have the vaguest idea what he meant, but he smiled, so she smiled too, marveling that here she was, having a real live conversation with Twig Lorimer. All she had to do was try and not focus on his incredibly wonderful smile, act like he was Joe Shmoe, and it was a snap!

"Oh, look!" Joss said suddenly. "There's my mother."

A crowd at the front door quickly encircled Mom and the professor, who looked exceedingly embarrassed by all the hubbub.

"Hey, Ma. *Ma*. Here we are," Joss said when she managed to get within shouting distance.

"Why, it's Jocelyn, isn't it?" Professor Macdunna poked Mom and then pumped Joss' hand. He looked very red in the face and kept wiping his forehead with a rumpled white handkerchief.

Mom hugged Joss. "Wasn't it terrific? I think it went wonderfully. And the audience was enthusiastic. *Very* enthusiastic. Don't you think?" Her mother never gushed, but she was gushing now.

"Dorothy, don't go forcing words into the poor child's mouth."

Mom was craning her neck to see past the crowd surrounding them. "Your father isn't here." She said it so matter-of-factly that it was impossible for Joss to tell whether she was upset or not. "Well, I'm glad you came," she said briskly. "And you too, Twig. Are your parents here?"

"Nope. They're away. But my sister is floating around somewhere."

"That's nice," Mom said distractedly. Already she was focusing on the next throng pressing in to meet the professor.

"So that's where you get those eyes from," Twig said a moment later, after they had settled themselves on the sofa.

"I guess so," Joss murmured, barely pausing to consider whether that counted as a full-fledged compliment or not.

She was watching Mom talking with Professor Macdunna. She looked so animated, gesturing, laughing, pausing to listen to what he said.

Joss turned away, suddenly feeling as if she was spying.

It was well after twelve o'clock when Mom rounded up Joss and Twig, and by the time they dropped Twig off at his almost laughably big, white-columned house, Joss was sleepy.

"Ma, what's kitsch?" she asked, once they were alone in the car on their way home.

"Oh, you know. Something that's so corny and awful, it's kind of wonderful in its own way. Like that really loud Hawaiian sport shirt I found for Daddy at the Deerfield Flea Market for his birthday last year. And those little Kewpie dolls I have. With all the ridiculous feathers."

"And our house. Is that kitsch, too?"

Her mother thought about it for a second.

"Yes. That's a perfect example, I suppose."

Joss remained silent for a moment, picking a fleck of dry skin off her lower lip. Then she said, "Ma, you know what? I think Daddy may be jealous of Professor Macdunna."

"What!" For a millisecond Mom's eyes darted from the road to Joss and then back again. "How on earth did you go from kitsch to that?"

"Well, I just was thinking about the lecture tonight and how Professor Macdunna's such a big deal from a famous university with everybody falling all over the place, making a fuss over him. And here's Daddy, who doesn't even know if he'll have a job after next year."

"Oh." Mom paused. "I guess I see what you mean."

"I'm worried," Joss went on in a rush. "I think he may be facing a mid-life crisis."

"Joss, honestly. The things you think of to worry about."

"No, really, Ma. This is no joke. I read all about it in one of Fletcher's father's magazines. And Daddy fits perfectly. He's exactly the right age, and he's coming to a crossroads in his career. . . ." Joss stopped. She wanted to warn her mother without alarming her unduly. "We have to be real careful, because if we don't watch out, he might go ahead and do something rash. Something he'd regret." She let the words trail off darkly.

Her mother misunderstood completely. "Joss, if you actually think your father is about to kill himself over a job at Bronwyn College, then you need to have *your* head examined."

"I didn't mean it *that* way," Joss declared hotly. "But he could do something else. In this article it talked about Gauguin. He was a famous artist."

"Thank you. I happen to know who Gauguin is," Mom said sharply. A lot of times Daddy would explain literary references to her mother or tell her who famous people were. It drove Mom up a wall. She said even dimwits didn't like to be patronized.

"Well, anyway," Joss continued, "Gauguin ran off to Tahiti or someplace when he had *his* mid-life crisis."

"Somehow I can't picture your father in the South Seas," Mom answered drily. "He gets sunburned too easily."

That's right, Ma. Go ahead and joke. It's only your whole marriage that's up in the air. Joss folded her arms and stared at the streetlights whooshing past her. Of course Mom had a right to be pissed after the selfish, babyish way Daddy behaved tonight. But still . . . "Well, I'm worried," she reiterated.

"Honey, *I* worry about how much *you* worry."

"I can't help it." Joss leaned back against the headrest. "I just want everything to be okay."

"Don't we all." Then Mom said it again more softly. "Don't we all."

Her mother's voice sounded so sad and resigned that without warning the back of Joss' throat started to sting, and she felt her eyes filling up. She turned away and stared out the side window so she wouldn't have to look Mom in the face. There must be some way to keep life from going absolutely haywire, Joss thought. She remembered when she was little, each night she'd arrange all her stuffed animals at the foot of her bed just so. Then she'd line up her slippers on the floor exactly side by side, so that the tip of one wouldn't poke out beyond the other, not even a fraction of an inch. It was then and only then that she could curl up in bed, safe at last. Safe from what? Joss still wasn't sure.

Six

"That last slice of pizza was the killer." Fletcher groaned as they parked their bikes on the Longmans' front porch. They'd just ridden in the rain from Phil's, slowly and in considerable agony, after their usual Saturday lunch. Joss had set out for the pizza place with freshly washed hair and secret hopes of running into Twig. But alas! There had been no sign of him. As consolation, she had stuffed her face with Phil's famous garbage pizza.

"Six slices I can handle. No problem. But seven is tough, even for the kid," Fletcher conceded with a belch, gingerly patting the front of his T-shirt, which proclaimed "Living Legend" in silver sparkle lettering.

"Could you *please* not talk about f-o-o-d right now," Joss whispered pleadingly. "I think the anchovies are starting to revolt."

She began wriggling out of her dripping slicker, but Fletcher, stepping up behind her, said, "Here. Let me help you with that," and, taking the raincoat from her, hung it next to his in the pantry.

Let me help you with that? Normally Fletcher had the manners of a baboon. Joss shot him a wondering look, but he either didn't catch it or chose to ignore it.

Yup, Joss thought as she lugged herself into the kitchen. No doubt about it. The past couple of days Fletcher had been acting very weird. Weirder even than usual. For one thing, not once had he mentioned seeing her with Twig at the lecture hall the other night. That wasn't at all like Fletcher. But Joss figured if he wasn't going to bring it up, neither was she.

Then, too, instead of just showing up at her house today as he did every Saturday, Fletcher had made a big deal of calling up beforehand to ask whether she was "free." As if Joss had a problem squeezing him into her busy social schedule!

Joss collapsed into a kitchen chair and, groping under her Bronwyn sweat shirt, undid the top button of her jeans. There. She exhaled with relief. That was a little better. "Why why why do I do this to myself?" she wailed. "If you're a real friend, Fletcher, for my next birthday you can give me a muzzle."

Fletcher picked up the paper that was lying on the

table next to a half-full mug of cold coffee. Dad's from breakfast.

"Hey." Fletcher suddenly perked up a little. "*The Blob* is on now. It just started. Wanna watch? Maybe it'll take our minds off our stomachs."

Joss shrugged and hauled herself into the den, where she fiddled with the old set until the wobbly picture settled into focus.

Normally Joss could sit through any horror movie. The trashier the better. And *The Blob* looked pretty decent. It was about radioactive protoplasm that kept growing bigger and redder the more people it ate up. It was one Joss had never seen before. But today her heart wasn't in it. She felt restless. Itchy. Charged up.

Daddy, she knew, was having brunch with Miss Dixon from the English department. They were meeting to compare rumors. Evidently Miss Dixon had heard that *he* was definitely getting tenure, while Dad had it on fairly good authority that *she* was the committee's choice.

As for Mom, she'd been out since the crack of dawn—gone even before Joss was up—getting flowers, extra hangers, more furniture polish, all in preparation for the house tour tomorrow.

It was so relaxed in the house without them that Joss kept wishing they'd simply never come back. Ever since the lecture, they'd both been impossible, so maddeningly polite to each other that at times Joss thought she'd laugh or scream.

"Dorothy, have you seen my book bag?"

"I think it may be in the den, Charles."

"Thank you, Dorothy. I couldn't remember where I put it."

What was this business with their names all of a sudden? If they'd started calling each other Mr. and Mrs. Longman, they couldn't have sounded any more formal or distant. If only her mother would break down and make the first move—it was so unlike her *not* to—instead of letting Daddy slip further and further away.

Absently Joss traced the zigzag pattern of the rain thrumming against the windowpane while Fletcher remained transfixed to the tube, watching the giant red slime slurp up more innocent victims. Eventually the blue VW came up the gravel driveway. Joss watched her mother emerge and race toward the door, a raincoat thrown over her head, carrying a large shopping bag with a bunch of flowers sticking out of the top.

"Don't you two dare mess up this room," Mom warned, poking her head into the den a moment later. "I spent hours last night cleaning up."

Joss nodded, although her mother's words didn't even register on Fletcher. He was miles away.

"Watch out, you shmuck! Look behind you!" he kept shouting at the TV screen, but despite his best warnings, the blob managed to put away the better part of a city population before it was finally subdued.

The second the movie ended, Fletcher was up switching channels, seeing what else was on. "Got any munchies around? A little popcorn or some Fritos maybe?" Fletcher's recovery time from pigging out never failed to amaze Joss.

"Fletch-*er*, no!" she said quite adamantly. "I refuse to sit around vegging out in front of the tube all afternoon." It seemed imperative to get out. Away. "Let's *do* something for a change."

"Such as?"

"I don't know. . . . What if we call Laura and go over to her house?"

"Oh, swell idea. Then we could all trade makeup secrets and talk about what every well-dressed teen will be wearing this summer." Fletcher made a face. "Honestly, I don't know how you can be friends with anyone who wears *designer* jeans."

"Talk about superficial!" Joss snorted. "You'd like her if you got to know her."

Fletcher appeared unconvinced. "Your trouble, Jocelyn, is that you see the good side of everybody. You have to learn to be more discriminating."

"Yeah, that's exactly what I keep telling myself," Joss countered, and when he realized what she meant, Fletcher laughed.

"Okay," he said with grudging good humor. "Chalk one up for your side."

"Why don't we go up and poke around in the attic?" Joss suggested. "It's a perfect day for it."

90

"Gee, Jocelyn. Just the two of us? Alone up in the attic?" Fletcher pretended to hesitate. "How do I know if I can trust you?"

Joss threw him a withering look. "I promise I'll try to restrain myself, Fletcher," she said, and clicked off the TV.

Fletcher dutifully followed her up to the attic. "I know this probably won't sound flattering," he said as he picked his way through a pile of clutter. "But one of the first things I liked about you was your house. It's so different from mine. Casa Dwoskin has all the charm and character of a Holiday Inn."

Joss, who was perched on top of an old trunk, laughed and said, "God, it's been ages since we spent any time up here."

The dust made Fletcher sneeze violently several times. The familiar cramped stuffiness of the attic with all its old memories made Joss feel safe, sealed off. She felt the knot in her stomach begin to loosen.

"The diary's in its usual place," Joss told Fletcher. "I was reading it the other night. . . . I wish there was some way I could have known Millie, don't you?"

Fletcher reached for the diary. "Good old Millie," he said with some affection. "I haven't thought about her in so long." He began leafing through the worn pages. "Look. Here's the time she met Elliot at that party. . . . And here's where he kissed her for the first time."

"Dear diary,"

Fletcher began reading in a high, fluttery voice.

"I am the happiest girl in Higham. No, in all of Massachusetts! Elliot kissed me. He truly cares about me. It is more than I ever hoped for."

Fletcher made a gagging noise.

"Oh, cut it out, Fletcher. It's pathetic the way everything has to be such a big joke with you."

But that was all Fletcher needed to hear to make him turn the page and continue his high-pitched recitation.

"I will never talk to Clara's sister again,"

he chirped.

"Not ever. Weezie Staunton read my diary! Now she is spreading it all over town about Elliot kissing me. Elliot insists we announce our engagement right away even though it will be some time before we can get married."

Fletcher looked up. "Boy, was that an understatement. Can you imagine. A two-year engagement. And then the guy goes off and gets killed." Fletcher shook his head. "Not smart. Not smart at all."

"I think it's romantic," Joss asserted hotly. "Millie never loved anyone else. She carried his memory to the grave."

"Oh, give me a break!" Fletcher exclaimed. "Do you realize how long they knew each other and they never even *did* it. Not once!"

"You would think of that," Joss snapped.

"Can I help it if I'm a normal, red-blooded boy?" Fletcher grinned foolishly. He put down the diary and suddenly moved nearer Joss, so near that she could feel his still-garlicky pizza breath blowing against the hairs on her arm.

"Let's go through some of the other stuff," Joss suggested, suddenly uncomfortable. She started to hoist herself off the trunk.

"We can do that later." Fletcher grabbed for her hand.

"Ouch! That's where my stitches were! Will you watch it!"

"Sorry, I forgot," Fletcher said, still pulling Joss toward him.

"What do you think you're doing!"

"Oh, come on, Joss. Don't you want to see what making out is like?"

"Are you *nuts*?" Joss couldn't believe she was hearing this.

"I'm just curious is all."

"Well, forget it! Find somebody else to be your guinea pig."

"It's not like I want to do something perverted, for Christ's sake. People do it all the time. See!"

Fletcher gripped Joss by the shoulders, pushed her down to his level, and rammed noses with her while planting his mouth on hers. There was a brief sensation of wet, slippery lips before Joss was able to shove him away. She wiped her mouth vehemently on her sleeve. "You are really gross. You know that? You are a total gross-out!"

"Well, excuse me, Snow White." Fletcher was breathing heavily, his eyes wide behind his glasses. He seemed as shocked as Joss by what had just happened. "I bet if it was Twig Lorimer, you wouldn't be putting up such a stink."

"Twig Lorimer has nothing to do with this," Joss shouted, jumping up and knocking over a tower of old hatboxes. "Just because I don't want your grubby little paws all over me—" she began, but then stopped. Fletcher looked like he might hit her or else burst out crying. He turned and pushed Joss aside.

"Hey, wait, Fletcher. Please!" *What was happening?* "I didn't mean it that way."

But Fletcher was already down the ladder to the second-floor landing. Joss scrambled after him. Damn her hand. She wasn't fast enough. Fletcher was taking the stairs two at a time to the first floor. Then— SLAM!—he was out the front door.

Joss slumped against the attic ladder just as her mother popped her head out of the bedroom. "What's all the commotion?" she asked. Joss burst into tears.

Mom came out, put her arm around Joss' shoulder, and handed her a Kleenex. Then she smoothed Joss' hair off her forehead. "Want me to just leave you alone for a bit?"

Mom was so good that way. She never pried.

Managing a watery smile, Joss honked loudly into the Kleenex. "Fletcher and I just had a fight. It was

94

dumb." How could she tell her mother that Fletcher had turned into some kind of raving sex maniac?

Mom patted Joss' face. "Don't look so miserable. You and Fletcher have been friends since you were eight. Do you honestly think one more fight is going to matter?"

Joss almost said she wished she was eight again. She'd been so much happier then. Why was it that everything seemed so complicated now?

Glancing at her watch, Mom frowned. "I didn't know it was this late. Listen, honey, I had some other errands I was supposed to run." Her mother looked like she was making up her mind. "But I can stay here with you. . . . I'll tell you what. You can help me clear out the hall closet for tomorrow. Okay?"

Joss nodded and headed for the bathroom. While she splashed cold water on her face, she could hear her mother dialing the phone. She was talking in a low voice. It sounded like she said, "I'm sorry but I can't make it. Something has come up at home."

There was the click of the receiver on the hook and then a few moments later, Joss heard Mom calling up to her from the front hallway, "Okay, honey, let's get cracking."

"Who was that?" Joss asked, as she came downstairs. Her mother didn't answer. She was already busy tossing out old bent wire hangers from the dry cleaners'.

The closet was a disaster area bulging with a collection of old parkas and coats; ski poles of varying sizes;

95

stray woolen gloves and linty scarves; lampshades un-
attached to lamps; a terminally ill transistor radio;
partial rolls of wrinkled gift wrapping paper; a gro-
tesquely obese clay cat with one ear chipped off, made
by Joss in second grade; a tennis racket missing half
its strings; a couple of small Tonka trucks that probably had belonged to Fletcher at one time; and, way
up on the top shelf, under a stack of yellowing issues
of the *Bronwyn Bugler*, a large brown manila envelope
labeled "Old Snapshots."

Eagerly, Joss opened the envelope. A tiny two- or
three-year-old Joss squinted quizzically at the camera
from atop Daddy's shoulders; a self-conscious Mom
held a hand over her face, as if she'd been caught
by surprise. In another, Daddy was stretched out on
a picnic blanket with his shirt off, holding a can of
beer. But the prizes of the collection were a seemingly
endless series of Mom pregnant with Joss.

Mom looked positively beautiful, radiant, glowing
with happiness—from the first pictures, where she appeared to be only a slightly more rounded version
of herself, to the final ones, which were almost a joke.
It honestly looked like her mother had stuffed a water-
melon under her clothes.

Funny, Joss thought, sitting down and going
through the pictures a second time, Mom didn't seem
at all embarrassed here. She'd even let Daddy take
one snapshot of her lying in bed, stark naked. "D-
Day minus three weeks" it was captioned in Daddy's
scrawly handwriting.

Joss felt her throat tighten. It killed her how happy Mom looked and how excited Daddy obviously had been. Why couldn't everything have stayed that way?

"Mom, look," Joss said.

"One sec." Mom was finishing dusting off the shelf. She pushed a strand of hair off her forehead with the back of her hand. "What is it?"

"Bet you forgot these were around." Somehow it seemed important for her mother to see the pictures. With a flourish, Joss fanned them out in her hand, as if she was presenting some vital piece of evidence.

Mom bent down and took the pictures. She glanced from one to another. At first she looked surprised; then her face settled into a sober, unreadable expression.

"One baby having another," her mother finally said quietly. She stared at the pictures again. "Well, I certainly hope you'll be a little smarter than I was when you're nineteen."

"Ma!" Joss yelped. "How can you say that! Didn't you want me?" Maybe that was it. Maybe everything had been perfect until she came along. Then goodbye romance. Hello diapers and baby doo.

Mom bit her lip and frowned. She looked as though she regretted saying anything in the first place, but she went on anyway. "Oh, I wanted you, all right. I wanted you desperately. But for all the wrong reasons." Then she tried to explain how, when she had dropped out of Barnard and married Daddy, part of her was rebelling against her parents and the establishment.

"The establishment!" Joss exclaimed, bewildered and upset. What did that have to do with anything? "I don't get it. You make it sound like Mobil Oil or something actually cared whether you got married."

Mom sat back and tapped the photos into a neat pile. "I know it sounds silly," she said slowly. "But bucking the system was such a big thing back then. There were all the protests against the Vietnam War. Protests against the university, too."

Joss nodded. There was a framed picture in Daddy's office of him hanging out of the window of a Columbia building. A newspaper photographer had taken the picture, which had appeared in *The New York Times*. Daddy and some other students had taken over the building and thrown the professors out! It was all over some plan the university had to knock down a neighborhood park and build a big new gym. Joss couldn't imagine anything like that ever happening at Bronwyn, where there were still Friday-afternoon tea parties in all the dorms. Her father was always saying how the only time his students ever protested was when they got low grades, because all they cared about was getting into business school or law school and making a ton of money. It was pretty obvious he thought the old days were better.

"Anyway," Mom continued, "the way I felt I could best strike a blow at the system was to have a baby who would be raised on love. Not authority, the way I felt I had been."

Joss remained sitting on the floor, cross-legged, saying nothing for a moment. "I don't know, Ma. It doesn't make a whole lot of sense to me."

"Maybe that's what I'm trying to say . . . that it didn't make much sense."

"Still," Joss pressed on anxiously, "it all worked out okay."

"Of course it did," Mom said too hurriedly, scooping the pictures back into the envelope. "I got a great kid like you, didn't I?"

Joss watched while Mom began packing up junk into a carton. What about her father, Joss wondered. Just where did he fit into the picture? Just how did Mom feel about him? More than anything, right now, she wanted to hear how Mom had been so in love with Daddy, so nuts about him, that when she first found out where he lived, she sat for hours over a bagel in the coffee shop across from his apartment building, waiting for a glimpse of him just so she could rush out and pretend to bump into him on the street.

Joss wished Mom had never told her about her crazy hippy past. She wanted romance. Aching hearts. And, above all, a happy ending.

Mom taped the lid of the carton shut and began neatly rearranging the to-be-kept stuff in the closet. Joss made a halfhearted attempt to help.

What if Mom felt that she was stuck with Daddy

and her? The thought had never once occurred to Joss before. Certainly she spent enough time worrying about whether or not her father was content with his part of the deal. But her mother? Never.

Joss stared at Mom, whose blouse was coming out of her skirt as she stretched to put back the package of photos on the shelf. Was it possible, Joss wondered, to think that you knew somebody inside out, and yet, when it came right down to it, really know very little at all? The afternoon with Fletcher, too, came back with a rush. If that was so, it was so scary. That meant everyone was all alone with their secrets. Who was to say . . . maybe if her mother had her whole life to live all over again, she'd do everything completely differently!

Seven

"Just please tell me why you stuck our house on this tour?" Joss questioned her mother accusingly. She had almost said "this dumb tour" but thought better of it. "It wasn't like anybody forced you. It was all *your* idea."

It was Sunday morning, almost time for the first arrivals. Mom was peering down at an end table she was polishing for about the fortieth time, as if she truly expected to see her reflection suddenly smile back at her, the way the ads always promised. "The house is of historical interest to the town," she said absently, moving her dust rag around in perfect little circles over the scarred wood.

Joss groaned. "Oh, come on, Ma. Some poor guy

choked on a wishbone is all. That hardly changed the history of America."

"Well, I didn't mean it quite that way." Mom continued rubbing. "I just meant people find our house interesting. Everyone likes a good creepy story. There's no harm in that. Besides, I thought you were looking forward to this tour."

Joss didn't answer. Before she had found out how kitsch their house was, Joss had been looking forward to the tour. Sort of. It made her feel important to know their house was grouped together with mansions like the Lorimers'. But now she saw the house with different eyes.

"I mean, I could understand you putting our house on *display* like this if it was really gorgeous or something," Joss went on, draping herself over the back of the sofa. "But look at this place." She flung an arm out at the hodgepodge of living room furniture, mostly cast-offs from other relatives or "antiques" Mom had picked up at thrift shops. "People are going to come here and laugh."

"Enough, Joss," Mom said sharply, finally looking up. She thwacked her spray can of Lemon Pledge down on the table. "I am not about to debate whether this house should or shouldn't be on the tour. Not when people are going to start ringing our doorbell in fifteen minutes. . . . And I don't need you bugging me, either. I'm nervous enough as is."

"Sorry. Forget I said a word," Joss practically shouted, and marched off to her room. She was in a rotten mood—a revolting, disgusting, horrendous mood—and had been ever since the crazy episode with Fletcher yesterday.

Late last night, after spending half an hour nervously picking up the phone and then slamming it back down, Joss had finally worked up the nerve to go ahead and call Fletcher.

"Um, I just saw in the paper that there's going to be a Steve Martin concert in Springfield next month," she began. Fletcher thought Steve Martin was a riot. "I thought maybe I'd send in for tickets. . . . I figured you might want one, too."

All Fletcher said was no. Period. Nothing else.

Joss listened to the bored, impatient sound of his breathing into the telephone. Fletcher was not going to make this any easier for her. All right. There was no choice then but to take the direct approach.

"Fletcher, *please*. Don't be this way," Joss implored. "I feel terrible. Can't we just forget about what happened today?"

"Exactly what are you referring to?"

"You know." Joss became even more flustered. "Up in the attic." Then she got it. "Oh, I see! You mean it's already forgotten!"

"You catch on fast, Jocelyn." Fletcher's voice was heavy with sarcasm.

"Well . . . great!" Joss tried to sound cheerful.

"Look, I can't talk now. I have to take a shower." And Fletcher hung up even before Joss could say good-bye.

When the doorbell had rung earlier this morning, Joss had raced for it, hoping against hope that she'd be greeted by some goofy T-shirt with Fletcher inside it. He had promised to keep her company during the tour; he'd even bought a rusty old security guard's badge from Odds and Ends downtown especially for the occasion.

Joss opened the door.

There stood Phoebe Jackson. She had on navy running shorts and a gray sweat-stained Cranhurst T-shirt. Her long red hair, which practically appeared on fire the way the sun was hitting it, was pulled into a thick braid, and a terry cloth sweat band was wrapped around her forehead.

"Hi, Joss." Phoebe's chest was heaving, and she sounded out of breath. "I just went for a run over by the pond, and since I was so close"—Phoebe paused to wipe her beaded upper lip with the back of her hand—"I thought I'd stop by to see if your father was home. I really need to talk to him."

"I'm not sure if he's still here," Joss lied, wondering how anyone could look so grungy and so gorgeous at the same time.

Just then the door to Daddy's office opened and the voice of Bob Dylan filled the front hall.

> *Something is happening*
> *But you don't know what it is.*
> *Do-o-o-o you, Mr. Jones?*

If her father had played that song once, he must have played it a million times lately.

"I thought I heard you," Daddy said. "Wait just a sec." He ducked back into his office again, cut off Bob Dylan in mid-wail, then reappeared. "Where have you been hiding yourself?" he asked Phoebe. "I haven't seen you in a while."

"I know. I've been chained to my desk, writing a paper for Romantic Poets. It's a load of b.s., but still I've had to pull two all-nighters this week. Talk about wrecked." Phoebe groaned for emphasis.

"It's probably horrible of me, dropping in on you like this," she continued, skirting by Joss and coming into the front hall. "But I *have* to talk to somebody. I'm in a total panic over what to tell Harvard about next year."

"Count on me to play father confessor," said Daddy, and he closed the door behind them.

Twenty-seven minutes later Phoebe emerged. Joss knew because she'd kept close watch on both her father's office and the wall clock right outside, while she swept and reswept the same patch of floor. What was going on? It was awfully quiet in there. A vision of Phoebe and her father entwined on the sofa, kissing feverishly, kept insinuating itself—Phoebe whispering how awful she was coming to his house this way. His wife and daughter right outside. But she simply couldn't help herself. . . .

At one point when Mom breezed by, stopping to

straighten a Miro poster that was hung crooked, Joss pointed toward the office with her broom and, in a dark voice, informed her mother, "Phoebe Jackson's here."

"Oh." Mom stepped back, surveyed the poster, and realigned it some more. Then she said, "Honey, the floor here looks terrific, but why don't you give the front porch a fast sweeping?"

Joss felt like clobbering her mother with the broom. Maybe *then* she'd wise up. Mom was hopeless. Absolutely hopeless. Couldn't she see what was going on right under her nose?

A few minutes after Phoebe finally departed, her father left, too.

"Should anyone inquire," he said to Joss as he threw on his old corduroy jacket, "I am seeking the sanctuary of the Bronwyn library for the day."

A likely story, Joss thought. She felt like telling her father that just because Mom was a total fool didn't mean *she* was, too.

"Give my regards to the thundering hordes," Daddy called out as he left.

There were no thundering hordes.

It was Joss' guess that, at most, thirty people came to see their house. Thirty-three if you included the jerky seventh-grade boys who kept reenacting Mayor Stillwell's death scene in the dining room, the "mayor" clutching his throat, gagging, and staggering around until he finally succumbed under the table. . . . Or thirty-four counting Professor Macdunna. Around noon, he "popped in" (his words) just to see how Mom was managing and to inform her that the volunteers from the Historical Society whom Mom had enlisted as guides in the other houses were "carrying on splendidly."

On his way out, the professor stopped by the front hall table to examine one of Mom's favorite knickknacks. It was a mechanical toy piggy bank, made sometime in the early 1900s. An old-fashioned mustachioed strongman with bulging metal forearms and a painted leopard-skin toga stood wielding a tiny sledgehammer next to one of those test-your-strength "thermometers" that used to be popular at amusement parks.

"It still works. Drop a penny in the slot," Joss told the professor.

He did, and the little strongman went into action, his muscle-bound body bending forward in small, fitful jerks until his hammer hit the base of the thermometer, sending a small red metal ball all the way up the column and down again.

"How did I miss seeing *this* before?" The professor laughed, exposing a funny space between his front teeth that somehow Joss had missed seeing before.

"I don't know. That bank is practically my mother's most prized possession. . . . She really goes in for kitsch stuff like that," Joss added. "But I guess you know that already."

"Indeed," the professor said slowly, turning the

bank over in his hands. His fingers were like the rest of him. Short and stubby. "Your mother has quite an extraordinary gift for seeing what's charming and lovable in funny old things." Then he put the bank back on the table and left.

The vast majority of the visitors did not share the professor's appreciation of Mom's taste. Ladies from church groups or garden clubs came and went, casting disapproving glances, just as Joss had expected they would, at the ragtag decor, raising eyebrows at the large bare spot in the living room Oriental rug, and clucking their tongues over the broken kitchen cabinet that Daddy had been promising to fix for months.

Joss stood woodenly in a corner of the living room, her arms folded, her lips pressed tightly together. But Mom smiled away, playing hostess to the hilt, pointing out the ornate living room fireplace of real Carrara marble; the paneling in the den that old Phineas Mortimer had shipped all the way over from some estate in England.

How could Mom be so pleasant, so polite? Joss wondered. There was such a thing as being too nice, she decided. Then you were nothing better than a chump, a pushover.

"I don't understand," Mom stage whispered as she passed by. "I thought you'd be such a help to me today."

"That's me, all right. Mother's little helper," Joss said under her breath.

Her mother looked surprised. She gazed at Joss

thoughtfully. "What's bothering you, honey?"

"Nothing is bothering me!" Joss exploded. "Everything is just dandy!" And for the second time that day she stormed off to her room, where she stationed herself on her bed and, reclining imperiously, glowered at anyone who peeked in from the hallway.

That's where she met Mrs. Trilling.

"If I don't use the toilet," the skinny old woman cheerily informed Joss, "I'm going to wet my pants."

Momentarily taken aback, Joss merely shrugged and said, "It's right down . . ."

"Oh, I know where it is," the woman said. "I used to come here often when I was a child."

In spite of herself, Joss became interested. She waited for her visitor to come out of the bathroom.

"Were you friends with Millicent Mortimer?"

"Eventually." Mrs. Trilling took in the posters of Bruce Springsteen on the walls and the menagerie of stuffed animals on Joss' bed. "This room is certainly different now," she said. "Millie had the most elaborate four-poster bed, with a canopy over it and heavy maroon tasseled draperies."

"The look is strictly early flea market now," Joss said.

Mrs. Trilling pushed back the polka-dot curtains and looked out on the dense fan of elm branches. "I always liked this room. . . . Never had a room of my own—that is, not until after my husband died— and I always thought this was the most wonderful private place in the world."

"Me, too. With the tree right outside you almost feel like you're living in a nest." Joss paused. "Millie once said this room was her 'hideout,' and I know what—"

"How on earth," Mrs. Trilling interrupted, "do you know what Millicent said about *anything*?"

Joss flushed, realizing her blooper. "Uh, it's a long story," she stammered. "Well, actually it's not such a long story. Millie kept a diary, and I sort of read it."

"Ha! Now if that isn't a coincidence. I've read it, too!"

"No kidding!" Joss exclaimed. "That makes me feel better. If Millie let you read it, then—"

"Oh, but I didn't say she let me, did I?" Mrs. Trilling lowered herself gingerly into Joss' rocker. "No, I most certainly did not have Millie's permission." Mrs. Trilling chuckled. "You see, Millicent and my sister never paid me a scrap of attention. Only reason my sister brought me over here was because Mother wanted me out from under. . . . I was a handful, let me tell you." Mrs. Trilling rocked back, seeming pleased with her former self. "Well, one day I saw Millie's diary on her nightstand. She and my sister were downstairs having lunch. So I sneaked back up here and read it. Millie caught me, too. Red-handed. But not before I got to the good part about her kissing Elliot."

Joss lit up. "Wait a minute. Are you Weezie Staunton?"

"Sure am. Or was before I got married. Of course, now everybody who used to call me Weezie is out in the Druids Lane cemetery."

"Weezie Staunton. Right here, talking to me," Joss marveled, trying to square her image of a bratty little kid with the slightly hunchbacked old lady before her. "Brother, you should see some of the stuff Millie said about you. She was really sore."

"Guess she had a right to be after I went and spread it all over town what she'd been doing with Elliot Bender! Of course I made it sound a lot juicier than it really was. Millie wouldn't talk to me for ages. But then in later years we became friends. Good friends. It all seems so silly now. Such fuss over nothing. Times certainly were different."

"Sometimes I wish I had grown up then," Joss found herself confessing. "There's this painting I really like in the Bronwyn museum of people skating on the pond a long time ago. The girls all have on long skirts and muffs, and everybody looks so happy."

"Oh, twaddle!" Mrs. Trilling said dismissively. "You're a fool if you think growing up was any better then. So many rules. So many lines you couldn't step over."

Joss wasn't at all sure that would have bothered her. "You don't know me," she said. "When I was little, I was the kind of kid who practically had a heart attack if I went outside the lines in a coloring book. I think I like boundaries."

"Well, aren't you a strange girl!" Mrs. Trilling observed, only the way she said it made Joss feel flattered.

"Hey, would you like me to bring some of Millie's old dresses and hats down from the attic?" Joss asked. "You'd probably recognize them. The diary is up there, too," she added with a smile. "I keep it in a special place."

"Some other time." Mrs. Trilling rose from the rocker with a slight wince. "No doubt the friends I came with will want to be heading on." She extracted a scrap of paper from her purse and found a pen in the mug on Joss' desk. "Here's my address. I have old photos of me and Mill and Clara. Even one or two, I bet, of Elliot Bender. You come by sometime and I'll show them to you."

"I'd like that." Joss put the address into her desk drawer. "I've never seen any photos of Millie. And I feel like I know her so well. Her cousin took all the family albums. I figure she would have taken the diary too if she'd known about it."

Mrs. Trilling smiled. "Well, I'd say Mill's diary probably landed in the right hands."

It would have been so much fun to tell Fletcher all about Weezie Staunton and plan when they would bike to Deerfield, the next town over, to visit her.

Telling Laura simply wasn't the same.

"It was amazing," Joss enthused between sandy bites of spinach salad after school on Monday. Pencil-thin Laura had suggested a "nonfattening" snack at a new health food restaurant downtown, and Joss, not eager to bump into Fletcher at Phil's Pizza, was happy to oblige. "It was like meeting a character out of a novel. . . . Only about seventy years after the story has ended."

"Mmmm. Sounds neat." Laura's lips were stretched into a grimace as she painstakingly applied a fresh coat of "Perfectly Peachy" lip gloss that perfectly matched the peach-colored jumpsuit she was wearing.

"So where should we look first?" Joss asked. It was obvious Laura was only trying to appear interested in the Weezie encounter. The real purpose of this outing was to find a dress for Joss to wear to Bobo's party. Lately Laura had been lecturing Joss about how she had to put "more zip and vitality" into her wardrobe.

"You need to make more of a fashion statement," Laura kept insisting.

"I *am* making a fashion statement," Joss said in her own defense. "My statement is that I don't care much about fashion."

"Well, it's time you did," Laura asserted, and in the end Joss had agreed, so she got out her baby-sitting money plus a generous gift from Mom, who told her to get something special.

"I figure we can check out Thurston's first," Laura said as the waitress wrote up their checks. "And then maybe look in some of the boutiques by the college."

Thurston's Department Store, however, was a total loss. "Strictly polyester" was Laura's disdainful judgment as she marched grandly out of the store with Joss trailing behind.

Outside they ran smack into Fletcher and his mother.

"JOCE-lyn! And LAUR-a! We're in such a rush so we'll just say hello before we dash off," Mrs. Dwoskin said. "We're running into EVERYONE today! We just saw Fletchy's old piano teacher. Imagine. I thought she'd DIED! And the nice young girl who used to do my hair at Irma's Beauty Shop. She's pregnant now."

While Fletcher's mother blathered on, Joss tried for a relaxed smile but felt her face stiffen. How should she act—friendly so Fletcher would see how much she wanted to make up, or cool and aloof so he wouldn't think it mattered to her so much?

Laura looked embarrassed. But then she knew all about the "attic attack." She was the only living soul in whom Joss had confided.

"See? Didn't I tell you he likes you?" Laura had said on the phone when Joss had told her what had happened.

"Will you quit saying that!" Joss had practically shouted. "Fletcher is so sex starved, he'd go after anybody. And I happened to be the only body around." Joss simply refused to see any other explanation.

"I'm driving Fletchy over to the orthodontist's in Westfield," Mrs. Dwoskin was saying now, gesturing at a mute, impassive Fletcher. "His bite plate cracked, but I just have to dash into Thurston's first to pick up some new bras and—"

"Mother, I'm sure we're all fascinated by your underwear shortage," Fletcher snapped, "but we're late already. See you," he added to Laura, not Joss, and abruptly steered his mother toward the revolving door.

"Fletcher looked like he wanted to *kill* his mother," Laura said once they were out of earshot.

Joss said nothing. How long, she wondered, was Fletcher going to keep it up? Acting as if she was the carrier of some new improved strain of bubonic plague.

"Really, Mrs. Dwoskin's not so bad," Laura continued as they strolled up the street. "She's flaky, for sure. But she's not as horrible as Fletcher makes out. . . . At least she means well, which is more than I can say for *some* people." Laura's usually soft voice took on a harder edge whenever she made any reference to her mother.

"That's Fletcher for you," Joss said with irritation. "Always acting as if he's got it so much worse off than anybody else. Hey—" Joss stopped. "You've met Fletcher's mother before?"

Laura seemed to take a deep breath. She fiddled with the peach-colored ribbon in her hair. Then she turned to face Joss. "Yesterday Fletcher asked me over to his house," she said quickly. "That's one of the reasons I didn't stop by for the house tour."

"Oh," Joss replied, stunned.

"I was meaning to tell you in school today. Honest. I don't want you to be mad or anything."

"Mad? Why should I be mad?" Joss said it so loudly a little boy carrying a skateboard stopped and stared. She hated the way her voice was beginning to crack and tremble. But Laura was *her* friend. Not Fletcher's. That sounded babyish, but it was true. In a fight, Laura belonged on *her* side.

"Joss, come on," Laura pleaded. "Please don't be this way. You're making me feel like some kind of Arnold Benedict."

"That's Benedict Arnold. And you said it. Not me."

Laura looked miserable. "Don't you see? I feel trapped in the middle. Here you are, my absolute closest friend in Higham. But—" Laura hesitated. "I also *really* like Fletcher."

Joss caught the emphasis of Laura's last words. "Wait just a minute. Do you mean what I think you mean?"

Laura gave a helpless little shrug. "I can't help it," she confessed. "Lately I'm a total basket case whenever I'm around him. He's so smart and funny and he has—I don't know—a really unique style."

That was one way of putting it, Joss thought.

"I didn't even realize how much I liked him until you told me about Fletcher kissing you. I was so jealous. I kept wishing it was me."

I can't believe I'm hearing this. Joss just shook her head and said nothing.

Laura continued on in a rush. "Then when Fletcher called me yesterday and asked me over, I got all excited. I figured maybe you were right about him not really liking you and just being hard up."

"I *am* right about that," Joss stated emphatically.

"Maybe so, but Fletcher didn't make one single move," Laura lamented. "We just sat around and watched a salute to Lucille Ball on TV. I swear I saw six episodes of *I Love Lucy* in a row!"

Secretly Joss was glad. It was crazy, but she felt jealous. If Fletcher and Laura were suddenly a couple, where would that leave her? And it struck her now that she'd actually been happy the times Fletcher refused to go anywhere with her and Laura. Deep down Joss wanted to keep them both for herself.

Still, Joss couldn't help feeling sorry for Laura. She looked so upset. "He's probably afraid to come near another girl after I went so bananas," she said.

"Or else he may have asked me over just to get back at you. Just to make you feel left out."

Joss sighed. If that was Fletcher's intention, he had succeeded.

"No, Laur," she said. "Not that I put it past Fletcher to try and get back at me, but I honestly can't see him using you that way. . . . Fletcher wouldn't pull something that low."

"Yeah? You mean it?" Laura seemed cheered. "Then maybe there is hope for me yet. Just please say you're not mad at me, Joss. I couldn't stand it. You don't know. I felt like such a rat, not telling you before. But I was scared. I didn't know how you'd take it."

"Well, I'm not mad," Joss said with a frown. "I don't know how it makes me feel exactly. But I'm not mad, I guess." After all, it wasn't like Laura went and picked out Fletcher to have a crush on. As for Fletcher, well . . . Had it been an act, all the times he referred to Laura as a mental midget, saying she gave primates a bad name? Had he been nuts about her all along? Joss sighed, feeling baffled. She was beginning to wonder if it was possible to fathom *anyone's* behavior.

They rounded the corner onto a double row of once-shabby frame houses that had recently been renovated into trendy shops and restaurants catering to the Bronwyn crowd.

All of a sudden the thought of shopping seemed more than Joss could handle.

"Laura, would you mind if we did this some other day? I'm just not in the mood right now."

Laura looked stricken again. "Joss, you *are* mad! Oh, I could kill myself!"

"That's not it. Honest," Joss paused. "I don't know. . . . I guess I can't see how some dumb dress is going to get Twig to like me." He'd been so nice the night of the lecture, but he'd barely said two words to her since.

"*Joss*, that is exactly the *wrong* attitude." Laura stamped her foot. "The idea is that you are going to look so fantastic at Bobo's party that Twig won't even remember her last name after he gets a load of you! Now come on."

Joss shrugged. She didn't have the heart to argue.

For the rest of the afternoon she let herself be escorted from boutique to boutique. From the start, she felt the outing was doomed to failure. Even dresses that looked absolutely great on the hanger lost all appeal once she put them on. "Why did God have to invent big hips?" Joss wailed as she struggled to get into a two-piece knit dress. "Please, can't we call it quits?" Perversely she found herself yearning for a double-dip cone of mocha almond fudge.

But Laura was stern. "We can't stop now. There are loads of places we haven't even hit yet."

Joss couldn't get over how tireless Laura was; Laura who practically had a heart attack if Ms. Hinkle had her run half a lap in gym class.

"Here, try these on," she commanded in the next store, shoving an armful of outfits at Joss.

"Uh-uh. I don't think that's really *you*," she conceded when Joss emerged in a puff-sleeved egg yellow dress with lots of big blue polka dots.

"I look like an overgrown blueberry muffin," Joss lamented.

But finally Laura did find *the* dress. It was short sleeved, with a bow that tied at the neck. The silky fabric was a soft green-blue, splattered with different colors all over, almost as if confetti had been thrown on it. From the second Joss saw it, she had a feeling the dress would be perfect.

"Ta-da!" she said, emerging from the dressing room, turning to give Laura the full effect. "Of course you have to picture it *without* the Nikes."

"It's *very* French," Laura breathed. The highest compliment in her book. "And the color is great with your eyes."

"You're sure it doesn't make me look fat? . . ."

"*No!*"

"Or too busty?"

"God, Joss. We should all have your problem."

Joss examined the price tag fluttering under her armpit. Then she bit her lip. "I don't know. It's kind of expensive."

"That's the last one in your size, and we won't be getting more in," said a saleswoman, who had suddenly materialized by her side.

"Oh . . . I'll take it!" Joss said, happily bowing to pressure, and on impulse she gave Laura a squeeze. "You were super to take all this time. Really. I'm so glad you made me come. I just hope Mom doesn't collapse when I tell her the price. . . . I've never bought anything this major without her."

"She'll love it," said Laura breezily. "I think I'll just pop into Rings 'n' Things next door while you pay."

A few minutes later, Joss found Laura mooning over a display case of earrings.

"Aren't they beautiful?" Laura pointed to a delicate pair of gold hoops.

"But you don't have pierced ears."

"I know," Laura sighed. "I'm dying to, but I'm just such a chicken. When I think of a needle being stuck through—"

"Don't even talk about it." Joss shuddered.

"The other week I almost worked up the nerve," Laura went on. "My dad was going to take me to Dr. Oglethorpe, but he won't put in studs. The only way he'll pierce your ears is with surgical thread. No way am I going to walk around for weeks with strings in my ears!"

"You know there's a girl in the tenth grade who pierces ears for three dollars and fifty cents, and she'll put in whatever you want."

"No kidding!"

"Yeah, you just have to have the earrings already."

"That's no problem," Laura said. "I have two pairs of gold studs from my two best friends in California. They both gave me the same present when I left." Laura leaned over the counter again, but she didn't seem to be focusing on the jewelry anymore. There was a glazed far-off look in her eyes. "Joss," she whispered in a hushed voice, "what if we *both* went and had it done *together*?"

Joss smiled weakly. "I had a funny feeling that was coming. But they are our ears after all," she reasoned. "I suppose we should be able to do what we want with them."

"It's all set," Joss said later, as she hung up the phone. "This Wednesday at four thirty. Sharon made me swear up and down we wouldn't ever breathe a word to our parents about who did the job."

"That's only fair."

"Oh, and her price went up. It's four fifty now," Joss added as she led Laura up to the attic.

It was only five thirty. Mom wasn't home yet, and Joss sensed Laura was not eager to leave, as if she needed some more reassurance Joss was still her friend.

"This is wild!" Laura exclaimed as they unearthed a dusty box of stiff petticoats and embroidered hankies and silk scarves and leather gloves, the kind that buttoned up all the way up past your elbow.

"I knew you'd freak." Joss opened a rusty steamer trunk. "And this isn't even the good stuff. Millie's cousin took all that. Whatever was left she said was ours, including that little vase." Joss pointed to a small brass urn perched on a stack of musty books. "Inside are Phineas Mortimer's ashes. He was Millie's father."

"Don't gross me out!"

"I'm not kidding, Laura. Millie's cousin didn't want them. And Ma didn't know what to do. . . . It seemed mean to throw Phineas away, so we just keep him up here—ouch! This stupid trunk." Joss waggled her pinched fingers, but at last it was open.

One by one Joss took out Millie's dresses. There was the pink with the high lace-trimmed neck, a purple-grayish check with a white sort of pinafore, and Joss' favorite, an ice-blue satin with tiny pearl buttons up the back.

"Oh, Joss!" was all Laura managed to get out.

"It's too bad they got all those terrible rust stains, but still you can imagine what they once looked like." Joss held out the blue dress. "Here. Try it on."

Laura wriggled out of her jumpsuit and into the dress. Joss helped with the buttons. "This is the dress Millie wore to the party where she first fell in love with Elliot Bender. In her diary she calls it her 'Alice Blue Gown.' That's because Alice Roosevelt, who was Teddy Roosevelt's daughter, always wore this color and made it very popular. There was even a song called 'Alice Blue Gown.' Ma explained it all to me."

Laura was not listening. She was too busy twirling around in the dress, which made soft rustling sounds as she moved. "Imagine wearing something like this! I feel like Vivien in *Gone With the Wind*."

Joss showed Laura the diary. It caught her interest more than Joss had expected, especially the parts where Millie talked about having no mother.

"Listen to this," Laura said, perched on the trunk.

"Today was Mama's birthday. She would have been forty years old. Papa spent the whole day alone in the library."

Laura stopped for a moment and seemed to be rereading the last part before she went on.

"I think I remember her singing lullabies at bedtime. Then other times I am not sure. Perhaps I only think I remember. Perhaps it is only that I have heard Papa

123

mention so often how she would sing me to sleep. How awful it is to have only other people's memories.''

Laura shut the diary. "I don't know if Millie was right," she said slowly. "I think it's better to have nice memories, even if they're somebody's else's, than crummy ones of your own."

"Don't you have *any* good memories of your mother?" Joss asked.

Laura stood and started to get back into her own clothes. "Not a whole lot. The only thing my mother ever gave me was this." Laura pointed to the hook in her nose. "And I plan to get rid of it as soon as possible." Then Laura said matter-of-factly, "Did you know I was only five when she left? She told me it was because she needed 'more space.' I thought that meant all we had to do was move to a bigger house and everything would be okay. I also remember my mother telling me the divorce had nothing to do with me." Laura rolled her eyes toward the attic ceiling. "Yeah, right—she decides she doesn't want to be married or be a mother anymore and it has nothing to do with me."

"Do you ever see her now?" Below, Joss could hear the front door slamming. Mom must be home. She thought of shouting down hello but didn't.

"Oh, sure. I have to visit her every summer for a few weeks out in California. She lives with this guy now who gets stoned a lot and talks about 'mellowing out.' What a jerk! I think he just stays with her because it's free rent." Laura zipped up her jumpsuit, smoothed her hair, and handed back Millie's dress to Joss. "I'm glad she's so far away. I'd just die if anybody around here knew what an idiot she is."

Joss remained silent, cross-legged on the attic floor, folding the dresses before putting them back in the trunk. There were times—and this was one of them—when she felt very childish next to Laura.

"Hey, listen," Laura said quickly. "I hope you don't mind me boring you with my *très* pathetic family history."

"Laur-a! Don't say that. I'm glad you feel you can tell me stuff like that."

"You're so lucky neither one of your parents are wackos. That time I had dinner here I kept thinking how normal everything seemed. . . . It made me jealous."

Joss didn't answer for a moment. *Stick around, then see what you'd say*, she was tempted to reply. But instead Joss found herself nodding in agreement and telling Laura the story of how Mom first met Daddy. "She and Daddy were both at a protest march against the war in Vietnam," Joss began dreamily, still holding Millie's soft blue dress in her lap. "The police came to break it up, and Daddy grabbed Mom just before some college kids got into a fight with the cops. Daddy ended up getting punched in the eye." Joss paused. That part was so wonderful. Daddy protecting Mom from the angry crowd.

Warming to her story, Joss went on to explain how

her father had had a girl friend at the time, "so Ma didn't think she had a prayer. She thought they were just friends. Until one day when they were studying in the library together, and Daddy leaned across the table and kissed Ma. Then he said, 'I love you.' Real loud. Right in the middle of the library. Right in front of a zillion people."

Joss sighed. The longer she talked, the better she felt. It was as if she was reciting some special incantation that would ward off evil spirits, stop anything bad from happening. It was stupid, of course. Like refusing to step on a crack in the sidewalk when she was little.

"That's so romantic," Laura murmured finally. "Like Ali and Ryan in *Love Story*. Only with a happy ending." Then Laura glanced at her watch. "Oh, Joss. I didn't know it was so late. I'd better go."

Joss nodded, closed the trunk, and started down the attic ladder, steadying it for Laura. "Listen, maybe on Saturday you could sleep over—that's if you don't have other plans."

Once again Fletcher seemed to pop up between them, making Joss feel awkward.

"Oh, no. I'd love that," Laura was quick to assure her.

"Good, then—"

Halfway down the ladder, Joss froze. The sound from her parents' room. Even with the door closed, there was no mistaking it. It was crying. Mom crying.

Joss' mouth went suddenly, horribly dry. Her

mother obviously didn't realize anyone was home. What had happened? It had to be something to do with Daddy. Had Mom finally realized she was losing him to Phoebe? Or maybe she'd suspected right from the start and had been pretending everything was all right for Joss' sake.

Wide-eyed, Joss placed a finger to her lips for silence, and very slowly and quietly she and Laura continued down the stairs, through the hall, and out of the house. Neither one of them said a word until they reached the pond at the end of the street, where Joss sank down on the grass. She stared past Laura to the island that sat so peacefully, like an egg yolk, in the middle of the pond.

"Poor Mom," Joss said, trying to keep her tone light. "She had a really big exam today. I guess she thinks she blew it." The phony sound of her voice made her want to hide. Who did she think she was kidding, anyway? "Plus she's nervous about Daddy's job. He may not get to teach at Bronwyn after next year."

Laura looked confused. "Joss, it's okay. You don't have to explain anything to me."

Joss nodded glumly, feeling miserable. A couple glided by in a canoe. The girl was lying back, a pair of sunglasses perched on her head, soaking up the last of the afternoon sun, while the boy pulled his paddle through the glassy water. They looked so happy. Joss wondered if it was the same couple she and Fletcher had surprised on the island that night.

Could that really only have been about two weeks ago?

Nervously, Joss shredded up handfuls of grass. Finally Laura got up and made a big deal of brushing dirt off her pants.

"Well, I guess I'll go. Dad'll be wondering where I am," she said.

Joss nodded again and watched Laura disappear down the street. She wanted to call out after her and tell her everything. How she was terrified Daddy was in love with Phoebe Jackson and that poor Mom would be left all alone in the lurch. But she was scared to say all that stuff out loud, as if once the words were out, they would hit the air and turn solid. As long as she said nothing, she could still hope. Maybe her fears had no more substance than a puff of smoke.

Eight

The bell from the steeple of the toothpaste-white First Presbyterian Church on Main Street chimed one . . . two . . . three . . . four times. Joss got a move on; Laura would already be waiting for her in front of Phil's Pizza.

It was Wednesday. The big day. Marked with an ominous red X on the Miss Piggy pinup calendar that Fletcher had given Joss last Christmas.

"Now remember. I'll meet you at four. At the pizza place. And puh-lease don't chicken out on me" were Laura's last words as she departed for Phil's with a bunch of other kids.

"I'll be there. I'll be there," Joss had muttered as

she trudged off for her appointment with Mr. Dupee, their English teacher.

It was weird sitting on the stiff wood bench in the hall outside the teachers' offices. Death Row was what the kids called it, because no one ever sat around waiting for good news. It was the first time Joss had ever been here.

Today when she'd failed to hand in the composition on Robert Frost's "The Gift Outright" that Mr. Dupee had assigned about two weeks ago, he'd looked at her quizzically and said to see him after last period.

As she worked doggedly on a hangnail, Joss saw Michelle Kline coming down the hall.

"What'd *you* do to wind up here?" Michelle said in surprise. She plopped down on the bench next to Joss, letting her stack of books land with a thud on the floor beside her.

"I didn't hand in a paper for Dupee."

Michelle pulled a strand of hair across her eyes. "My, my, my," she said, while searching for split ends, "that certainly doesn't sound like the Joss Longman we all know and love."

Joss gave Michelle a sick smile. "Yeah, well, I've had other things on my mind." *That* was a mild understatement, although Joss wasn't about to go into it with Michelle. The Mom-Daddy business had her so preoccupied that Joss had totally forgotten about the English assignment until Mr. Dupee had asked Bobo to collect all the papers at the beginning of class.

"Well, don't sweat it, Joss. This is the *third* paper I haven't done for Dupee." Michelle giggled. "Of course, that's one of the good things about being in all the dummy sections. The teachers never really expect you to do the work." Michelle pinched the end of one strand of hair and artfully nipped off a split end. "Hey, Joss. Do me a favor. Let me see Dupee before you. Bobo's outside waiting for me, and if I go in first, Dupee'll get all his yelling out and he'll go easy on you."

"I'm sorry, Michelle. I can't. I'm supposed to meet—"

"Oh, come on." Michelle tugged on Joss' arm. "I have to help plan the food for the party on Saturday. And Bobo's going to be mad if she has to wait."

"Lookit, Michelle. I have to be somewhere, too." *Brother*, was Michelle pathetic. All that was missing was the leash.

"Well, thanks. Thanks a bunch," Michelle snapped, and turned away to search for more split ends.

A few minutes later the gray metal door to Mr. Dupee's office opened.

"I'll see you now, Jocelyn." Mr. Dupee motioned her inside.

Their meeting was brief.

From behind a desk overflowing with students' papers, Mr. Dupee sat back in his swivel chair, his fingertips pressed together into a little steeple. He gazed thoughtfully at Joss over the tops of his glasses. To her surprise, he asked if everything was all right, because she'd seemed so—well, so distracted lately. Joss assured him everything was fine, thank you, just fine, and that she was sorry about the paper but she'd had a lot of other work and would hand it in on Friday.

"That'll be okay," Mr. Dupee said. "And I'm glad to hear nothing's been bothering you." The way he said it, there was still a question in his voice.

Shifting in her chair, Joss smiled nervously. "Is it okay if I go now?"

Mr. Dupee nodded, and Joss made for the door. "Thanks for being so nice about the paper," she said, then raced down the hall. In a way she wished Mr. Dupee had really chewed her out so that she could feel angry now instead of guilty. Mr. Dupee was an okay guy. A tough grader but almost always fair, and it made Joss feel like a creep to lie when he seemed genuinely concerned.

Five minutes later Joss was hurrying down Main Street, past Caswell's Pharmacy and the bored-looking dummies in Thurston's windows, and—at the corner of the street—Dewitt Bros., Fine Jewelers. This was the turnoff. Four blocks down the street, in a crummier, run-down section of town, was Phil's.

The elaborate gilt clock above the door of Dewitt's told Joss it was almost ten past four, but the fourteen-karat gold goodies in the windows, lying on luxuriant beds of black velvet, held her for a moment.

Cupping her hands around her eyes to cut down the glare, Joss spotted a beautiful pair of pearl stud earrings, lustrous and creamy, twinkling up at her from the window. Of course they probably cost a mint. Everything at Dewitt's did.

Inside the store she could now make out a salesman showing something to a couple whose backs were turned to her. The man had on a beat-up corduroy sports jacket, like the one Daddy always wore, with a maroon book bag slung over his shoulder . . . like Daddy's. The woman, who was huddled close to him and pointing to something on the counter, had long hair—long, beautiful red hair—that was plaited down her back in a thick braid.

Daddy and Phoebe Jackson. It *was* them!

All of a sudden, Joss felt rooted to the sidewalk; she couldn't budge. It was them! She wasn't imagining it. What if Daddy and Phoebe Jackson turned around and saw her? Would they think she was spying? What would she do? Keep standing there and wave back?

Somehow Joss managed to pull herself away from Dewitt's and bolted down the block. Daddy and Phoebe. Daddy and Phoebe together. What were they doing? Picking out a wedding ring? No. No. That was crazy. Daddy hadn't even left Mom. . . . Not yet.

But it was going to happen. Joss was sure of that now. It was just a question of when. The ringing in Joss' ears subsided—she had not even been aware of it until it stopped—and a strange calm began to settle over her. There was some comfort in knowing the worst was true. Like getting back a test you'd been a wreck over and seeing your grade was as rotten as you feared. At least the worrying and uncertainty were over.

Mechanically Joss continued on to meet Laura. She felt as if she was walking on stilts. She tried imagining what it would be like for her and Mom to be alone, but all she could think of were those dumb commercials for life insurance where the father in the happy family suddenly fades right out of the picture.

When she turned the corner to Phil's, Laura was already outside waiting for her.

"Joss, are you all right? You look like you just saw a ghost."

That almost made Joss laugh. She wished it *had* been ghosts. "No, I'm okay."

"Was it *that* hairy seeing Dupee?"

Dupee . . . Dupee? It took Joss a moment to figure out what Laura meant. The image of Daddy and Phoebe Jackson kept flashing across her mind like instant replay. "Oh, *that*," Joss said. "It was nothing."

"Uh, listen. We really don't have to rush off for our appointment. We still have a little time. Want to have a Coke or something inside before we go?"

From Laura's hesitant expression, Joss could tell she expected her to put up a fight. Not since the day of the attic attack had Joss set foot inside Phil's. It was bad enough seeing Fletcher in school every day, where he acted as if she was starring in the remake of *The Invisible Man.* She didn't have to go looking for other places to run into him. Plus Joss wasn't sure she was ready to see Fletcher and Laura together.

When she was with Laura, just the two of them, it was almost as if Fletcher didn't even exist—neither one of them ever brought him up. But now all the evading and pretending seemed kind of ridiculous.

Joss shrugged. "Sure." And she followed Laura inside.

At the counter Joss gave her order and then carried her soda and buckling slice of pizza to a booth, where Laura sat with Fletcher, his head buried in the *National Tattler*.

"Greetings and salutations." Joss tried to sound natural as she slid into the booth.

Fletcher grunted, never lifting his eyes.

Laura giggled nervously. "Can you believe Fletcher? Actually reading that garbage. I think all the stories are made up anyway. Listen to this . . . 'Mother gives birth to twenty-five pound baby,'" Laura read over Fletcher's shoulder. "I mean, that's just not possible, is it?"

When neither Fletcher nor Joss answered, Laura glanced nervously at the Coca-Cola clock on the wall. "Ooh, Joss. It's almost time. I haven't told Fletcher where we're going," she added conspiratorially. "It's going to be a surprise." Then she stood up and gave a fake cough. "Um—well—I think maybe I'll just make a quick detour," she said, and exited toward the ladies' room.

What a cheap shot, Laura ducking out like that, Joss thought as she sank her teeth into the greasy pizza. Laura just wanted to get away from an uncomfortable situation. Nobody ever went into the bathroom at Phil's. Not on a bet. You could never find any toilet paper, and there was always a funny smell inside. Then it occurred to her that Laura might be leaving her alone with Fletcher on purpose. A little reunion! Of course, that was it. Well, too bad. It wasn't working. Fletcher was not even acknowledging her presence.

She reeled in a long, stringy piece of pizza cheese with her tongue and watched Fletcher reading. There was chocolate at the corner of his mouth. Fletcher was one of the few people who found Hershey's and mozzarella a perfectly acceptable combination. The sight of his smeared face made Joss sad. It reminded her of a snapshot she'd taken of Fletcher a couple of summers ago on a day when they'd rowed out to the island for a picnic.

It had been a very hot day, and Joss remembered lying in the sun, swilling soda and licking the melted remains of chocolate bars from their wrappers.

"What do you think is the most embarrassing thing that's ever happened to you?" Fletcher had asked out of the blue. Joss knew that no matter what awful incident she would relate, Fletcher was bound to top it. Still, she mentioned the time she threw up on Mrs. Werle, their third-grade teacher, and when her pants had split all the way down the back during rhythm class in the fifth grade. But it was obvious from the way Fletcher was shaking his head that he considered her humiliations strictly minor league.

"You're not going to believe this when I tell you . . . but first you have to—"

"I know. I know. Swear not to tell a soul." Joss had finished for him.

So Fletcher told her about his first piano recital at age six. "There I was in this spiffy little blazer and shorts with a clip-on bow tie and my hair all slicked down and I can see my mother and my father looking real nervous in the audience and my teacher, Miss Fishman, is smiling and pointing for me to start. So I sit down, and then just before I hit the first note, I let one!"

Joss stopped drinking her soda. "You didn't!"

Fletcher nodded gravely. "I did—and I'm not talking about any SBD—Silent But Deadly. I mean a real firecracker. L-O-U-D. It kind of filled the whole auditorium."

By this time Joss was so convulsed that some soda shot straight up her nose, and Fletcher had to pound her on the back before the choking subsided.

Now Joss sighed with regret as she watched Fletcher, with studied nonchalance, turn a page and casually pick his nose. It was a very quick gesture. Not even that gross, really. But it hit Joss that it was a typically Fletcher way of letting her know that for him, at least, she barely existed.

All at once a ball of fury knotted inside her. Up till now she had felt hurt and frightened that Fletcher could have turned against her. She had been willing to blame herself for not handling the situation better. But not anymore.

"I hope you're getting a big charge out of acting this way, Fletcher," she heard herself saying, "because it's not working on me. Not anymore. If you can treat me like this, all it means is that we were *never* friends. I was just somebody who was around, somebody you could talk into doing stuff *you* wanted to do." Joss glared at the top of Fletcher's head. He made no reply. But his eyes kept scanning the exact same spot on the page over and over again. "If you want to know the truth, it so happens I was sick of being your trusty little sidekick anyway."

With a certain majesty, Joss rose from the table. Her soda toppled. Although she managed to catch it before it crashed to the floor, some Coke sloshed over the table, seeping onto Fletcher's magazine and dripping down her skirt. Rats! Joss thought. She was wrecking her exit line. Nevertheless she squeezed out of the booth with as much dignity as she could muster, and grabbed Laura by the arm just as she was emerging, slightly green, from the bathroom.

"Come on, Laura. It's time to go." Joss grabbed her by the arm as she strode out of the pizza parlor. Laura had to walk quickly to keep up with her.

"It didn't work, did it?" Laura asked. It was actually less of a question than a statement of fact.

"No. But it was a nice try."

Laura sighed. "I hate all these hard feelings *sooo* much. God, how I wish you and Fletcher were friends again."

"I know." Joss managed a smile. "Only it's not going to happen. And to tell you the honest truth, I'm beginning not to care." Joss paused. "I mean it. I never *ever* thought I'd say that. But I mean it."

"It was dumb of me to stick my nose into it. I know that. But I just want everything to be—to be nice," Laura added lamely.

Joss nodded. As good old Dr. Dwoskin would have said, she could really relate to that. But sooner or later you had to face facts. Joss figured she could keep on wishing from now until doomsday that everything would be fine again between Mom and Daddy. But what difference would that make? Zero difference.

"Hey, listen, did you remember to bring the money for Sharon?" Laura asked, switching gears. "I've got both pairs of earrings right here with me." She patted her purse. "I still can't believe we're going through with this. Can you?"

Joss didn't answer. She gave Laura a long, hard look. She felt her throat go dry and her heart start to pound. She had to tell *somebody* what was going on with her parents. And Laura would understand. Joss sucked in a deep breath. Out with it, she ordered herself. "You know what, Laur. I'm really scared about—"

Laura didn't let her finish.

"Oh, Joss, Joss. I know. Don't you think I'm scared, too?" She held up a trembling hand in evidence. "I'm a wreck. All I can think of is this friend of mine who let a kid pierce her ears and it came out all crooked. The holes weren't in the same place. It looked awful."

Laura stopped dead in her tracks, terror stamped on her face. "I'd die if that happened to us. We'd look like such freaks!"

"Don't worry. That's not going to happen to us," Joss said quietly. In a way she felt relieved that Laura had not let her spill her guts out. . . . Maybe it was just as well. "This kid Sharon is supposed to know what she's doing."

Although Joss was nervous too, she was glad to have this mission ahead of her. It meant not having to think about anything else . . . at least for a little while.

When they reached Sharon's house, a plump girl in plaid Bermuda shorts answered the door.

"Hi, I'm Sharon," she said. "Everything's all ready downstairs. We'll have to hurry, because my mom will be home pretty soon."

Sharon's basement set-up was so professional-looking, it was almost creepy. Next to a fake leather reclining chair, the kind that Fletcher's father had in his office, was a table covered with a white sheet. On it, spread in neat array, were a mirror, bottles of rubbing alcohol and iodine, a bowl of ice, another smaller empty bowl, a bag of cotton balls, some rubber bands, a cork, a pack of matches, and deadly-looking sewing needles with thread dangling from them. Joss swallowed hard. All the paraphernalia was mystifying to her, but not to Laura, who informed Sharon that the thread wouldn't be necessary because they'd brought earrings with them.

"Fine," said Sharon. She was scrubbing her hands at the corner sink, the way surgeons on TV always did right before they went in for the kill. "Just drop them into the empty bowl. I'll pour some alcohol over them." Sharon came over to the table. She lit a match and held a needle in the flame. Then she looked straight at Laura. "Take a seat. And pull your hair back with one of those rubber bands."

Laura did as she was told and lay back in the reclining chair. Sharon took a cotton ball soaked in alcohol and rubbed Laura's ears all over. They looked so little, so pink, Joss thought, biting her lip. She watched as Sharon took the iodine dropper and made a neat dot in the center of each lobe. Like little bull's-eyes. After that Sharon held ice to Laura's ears until she said they felt numb.

"Okay. Here we go." Sharon was poised with the cork and sterilized needle. "This won't hurt a bit."

Joss clutched Laura's outstretched hand with all her might. Poor brave Laura! She couldn't bear to watch.

"*Ouch*!" screamed Laura. "You're killing me."

Joss nearly swooned.

"Are you nuts?" said Sharon. "I haven't even touched you yet!"

"Not *you*. Jocelyn. She's practically breaking my hand," Laura said with some irritation.

"Sorry," Joss mumbled, loosening her grip.

"Listen, the sooner we start, the sooner it'll be over and done with."

Laura nodded. This time she simply clutched the sides of the reclining chair.

The whole business was over in a flash. Suddenly there were twin dots of gold nestled in Laura's ears.

"How do I look?" she asked, peering anxiously into the mirror that Sharon presented.

"I got 'em dead center if I do say so myself. Okay, next victim," Sharon ordered cheerily, and Joss felt she had no choice but to sit down.

The horrid procedure was repeated step by hygienic step. There was no real pain, Joss had to admit, just a sickening little crunch as the needle jabbed through.

"Done!" Sharon announced.

"Thank God!" Dank and limp, Joss collapsed out of the chair and flung her arms around Laura in a wave of exultation and relief.

"We did it!" Laura cried joyously.

"I never could have done it without you. Not in a million years," Joss said with feeling.

They hugged each other hard.

"Hold it a second before you go," Sharon interrupted. "I've written down everything you should do so you won't get an infection." With a crisp rip, she tore off two pieces of notepaper and handed them to Joss and Laura. "If there are any complications, call me right away."

Upstairs, they paid Sharon and thanked her profusely. "You have the hands of a born surgeon," Joss said with genuine admiration.

"I know," Sharon replied, and closed the door.

Nine

Perfect timing. It was the morning of Bobo's party and overnight a brand-new pimple, red and bumpy, had blossomed smack in the middle of Joss' forehead.

"Somebody up there is out to get me," Joss muttered at her reflection in the bathroom mirror as she smeared on more acne cream. She wondered how a paper bag over her head would go with her new dress.

"Did you say something, honey?" Her mother passed by in the hall.

"What am I going to do?" Joss wailed, sagging against the sink and pointing to the ostrich egg on her forehead.

"About what?" Mom asked.

"Ma! It only looks like Mount Saint Helens is about to erupt!"

The blank expression on Mom's face did not change. But then, she had been in a total fog lately. She hadn't even noticed when Joss had arrived home, proud and defiant, with her newly pierced ears. In the end Joss had been forced to pull her hair back and point out what she'd done.

"Well, they're your ears," was all Mom said, leaving Joss feeling deflated and cheated, even though that had been *her* reasoning precisely.

Of course Mom had other things on her mind. It had to be eighty zillion times worse for her, waiting for Daddy to spring the news. Not that it was easy on Joss. No, it was like hearing someone take off one shoe. You could go bonkers waiting for the other one to drop.

And Daddy certainly was biding his time. The other night Joss couldn't believe her ears. In the middle of dinner her father had announced that he didn't even care anymore if he got tenure. That it wasn't the end of the world. Joss had nearly fallen off her chair. Of course it wasn't. Not when he had Phoebe around to follow him anywhere, even to Cretin U.

Mom came up closer to inspect Joss' face. "Oh, *now* I see what you're talking about. Don't worry, honey. It's nothing. With a little makeup you'll never see it."

Sure, sure, Joss thought.

There were still several hours to kill before going over to Laura's house. They were going to get ready for the party together, and afterward Joss was sleeping over.

Right now Laura was at Irma's Beauty Shop having a special manicure where they glued on plastic nails and then polished them so you couldn't tell they were fake. It cost fifteen dollars.

"Laur-*a*!" Joss had shrieked when she heard the price. "Think of all the stuff you could buy with that money."

"My three best nails broke off this week," Laura had countered. "And besides, I want to do it. It's *good* to be good to yourself."

"Oh, yes. I forgot. The Gospel according to *Glamour Teen*."

"Laugh if you want, Joss. But it wouldn't kill you to do something like that sometime. You have a crummy self-image."

Joss stood at the window, quietly watching a fat gray squirrel outside in the tree, nibbling on something that it held in its small paws. Oh God! How was she possibly going to survive until tonight?

Last night she'd had a dream about the party. From opposite sides of the room she and Twig had come floating toward each other, just like in a movie where everything suddenly goes all slow and misty. When he had reached her, Twig had murmured, "At last, we are together!" Then he had held out his arms to Joss, who, weightless and airborne as a humming-bird, had glided into them. But that was as far as the dream got.

Joss had woken up feeling disappointed and cheated. She tried to go back to sleep and pick up where she left off. But it was no use. Why was it nightmares always went on for years while the good dreams were over in a flash?

Fishing around in her closet, Joss found her overnight bag and began tossing shoes, shortie pajamas, clean underwear into it. What was the real-life Twig doing this very second? she wondered. Probably he was already at Bobo's, setting up all the stereo stuff for the party. Please, please, *please*, God, Joss prayed. Don't let him dance with her all night. Even if he doesn't like me, don't let him like her too much. Joss zipped up the bag. What if *nobody*, not a single soul, asked her to dance and she had to stand around all night, looking stupid, while everybody else had a good time. Oh God! That was probably *exactly* what it would be like. The eggs she'd had for breakfast began to lurch dangerously inside her. Was she going to throw up? Joss sank on her bed and gulped in air. Millie Mortimer had puked, Joss remembered, right before leaving for the Lorimers' fancy dress party, the night she met Elliot. In her diary she'd written how she almost ruined her Alice Blue Gown. Good old Millie.

In a minute Joss had the diary and was in her room again, leafing through the yellowed pages until she hit the entry she was looking for . . . May 24, 1916.

Dear diary, I woke up with a terrible headache this morning,

Millie had begun in her feathery script.

Mrs. James was worried it might be influenza, but it is just that I am so frightened about the party tonight.
This afternoon I took a long walk with Papa through the Smith Woods. It is so wild and beautiful out there.

Joss stopped reading for a moment, wondering what Millie must have thought when the woods became the Colonial Heritage development where Fletcher and Laura and so many other kids in her class lived.

All Papa talked about was how I must be on my very best behavior tonight. Then he said to remember that I am a Mortimer and I don't have to feel second to anybody. Oh, dear diary. I hope I won't disgrace myself tonight.

Poor Millie. Joss knew exactly what she was going through. But for Millie, at least, it had ended up being an evening straight out of a fairy tale. Joss turned the page. Nestled in the crack of the diary were the brown, dried-up remains of the rose that Elliot Bender had given her. Careful not to blow the bits of flower away, Joss read on.

Last night already seems like a dream. I can scarcely believe it all happened. But it did. I have the rose that Elliot gave me to prove it. Henderson drove Clara and me to the dance. I was sick to my stomach right before I left. How like me to do something like that! As soon as we arrived, a flock of admirers surrounded Clara, who was all in white.

But then, from the edge of the group, came a voice. "May I have this dance?" someone said so softly I almost didn't hear it. Clara said, "Why, Millie, I'm sure you won't say no to—Elliot Bender, isn't it?" And before I knew it, I was on the dance floor. We danced and talked and danced. A few times I found myself leading—horror of horrors!—but Elliot did not seem to mind.

He is from New York City, a cousin of Mrs. Lorimer's. In the fall he will be entering Harvard (Papa will like that!), but he is spending the whole summer in Higham! Tuberculosis nearly killed him this winter, and the doctors hope the country air will make him strong enough for college.

Oh, I could go on and on. How beautiful the Chinese lanterns looked in the garden. And what songs the band played. But I must go to sleep. It is already past three, and if Papa were to see my light on . . .

Joss closed the diary. It was weird thinking Millie had written all that over sixty years ago. Why, that was even before her own grandmother had been born! And now Millie was dead, dead for years, yet reading the diary made Joss almost feel that if she closed her eyes and then opened them, Millie would be standing before her—a girl not much older than herself. Dreamily, Joss lay back on her bed and, staring up at the whorl of plaster vines that trailed about her ceiling—Millie's ceiling—wondered if after tonight she too would have any memories to store away and keep forever.

"Pretty glamorous, huh?" Laura said, waggling ten flaming red talons at Joss. "The color is Temptress," she added with a giggle.

"Will those things really stay on?" Joss asked.

"They're guaranteed for a week, but I don't know. They do feel kind of weird." Laura waggled her fingers some more. "I may need you to help later with the buttons on my dress. Ooh!" Laura's mouth fell open. "I wonder if I'll be able to put on my eye makeup. I never thought about that."

"Don't look at me, Laur. I was counting on *you* to do a miracle job on *me*."

"Where there's a way, there's a will," Laura chirped happily.

Joss hung her dress in the walk-in closet. Once again she was struck by the vastness of Laura's wardrobe. It was like a small department store inside. "How can you be in such a good mood?" she asked irritably.

Laura bit her lip. "Oh—I feel funny saying."

Joss stamped her foot. "Laur-a! Don't be that way. Now you *have* to tell me."

"Wel-l-l," she began hesitantly. "It has to do with you-know-who."

Once again Joss felt a sick pang at the mention of Fletcher. Would that ever stop? she wondered. "Lookit, Laur. How long can we keep up this game of *not* ever talking about him? It's dumb. Besides, you're my friend. If you have a crush on someone, then I want them to like you back. Just 'cause it's Fletcher doesn't change that."

"You mean it?"

Joss nodded. She *wanted* to mean it. That was almost the same thing.

"Well, Fletcher called me this morning. To see what time I was getting to the party. It was like he was checking up, to make sure I'd be there. I think it must mean he likes me, at least a little."

"I bet he likes you more than that," Joss said.

"You think? Oh, I hope." Laura did a little dance around her room before collapsing on one of her twin beds. "Maybe tonight will be the night. Fletcher will suddenly look at me with a little smile on his face," she mused. "And then he'll kiss me. Finally kiss me. I swear, I've never wanted anything to happen so much in my entire life."

Joss collapsed on the other bed and turned toward Laura, hugging a pillow to her. "I'm petrified Twig will be with Bobo all night. I can just see it now. . . ." Joss swept out her hand for emphasis, nearly knocking over a plastic bowl on the end table between the beds. "Whoops!" Joss steadied the bowl, which, she noticed, was filled halfway to the top with some sort of gray-green muck. "Laura, what is this?"

"Oh, that. I'm glad you reminded me. It's a special Beauty Revitalizing Mask. I whipped it up this morning."

"Just so long as it's not lunch." Joss bent over and sniffed. "What's in here anyway?"

"Oh, all sorts of stuff. Avocado and bean paste and a little honey," Laura ticked off the ingredients on her fingers, "and some wine vinegar and a whole bunch of other things. I got it out of an article in *Glamour Teen* called 'Five Easy Steps to a Beautiful New You.' It's supposed to leave your complexion with 'a healthy, feeling-good glow.' You want to try it with me?"

"Sure, what have I got to lose? My skin looks like a Nestlé's Crunch bar."

Laura bounded out of the room and returned with a box of oatmeal and a wooden spoon. "This is the last ingredient. It said not to put it in until right before you're ready to apply the mask." Laura stirred in a generous amount. "We have to leave this stuff on for at least forty minutes, and while it's hardening we're supposed to lie down and think 'beautiful, serene thoughts.'" Laura surveyed the lumpy mixture in the bowl with a satisfied air. "There. Looks done to me."

"I'll smear it on both of us," Joss offered. "So you won't have to wreck your nails."

Laura spread two big bath towels over the beds. Then she lay down and let Joss slather her face. "You look like something out of *Revenge of the Mummy*," Joss said when she was finished. Then, scooping up another slimy handful, she went to work on herself.

"Ooh, this stuff stings!" she cried, scrinching up her face.

"Probably the vinegar," Laura mumbled from under the mask. "Forget it. Just lie back and be serene."

"Uh huh." Carefully, so she wouldn't drip on Laura's satiny pink bedspread, Joss lowered herself on the towel and closed her eyes. The zit on her forehead throbbed, and the smell of avocado was making her queasy again.

"Laura?"

"Ummmmm?"

"Do you think it will turn out to be a make-out party?" All week Bobo had been telling the world how her parents were under strict orders not to set foot in the basement anytime during the party.

"It better be." Laura giggled. "I'm counting on it. But you know more about the parties around here than I do."

"Party. Singular," Joss corrected. "There has been exactly one all year. Michelle gave it last Thanksgiving. She was the only one who asked me to dance all night."

Laura laughed. "Tonight will be better. I'm sure of it. You know, in California *all* the parties were make-out parties. The last one I went to before moving here was sort of in my honor. Like a farewell party. I was with that boy Pete all night. Remember, I told you about him."

"Yeah, the one whose cigarette butts you kept."

"That's the one." Laura sighed at the memory. "I

went farther with him that night than I've *ever* gone."

"Really?" Joss tried to keep her voice neutral. She didn't want Laura to think she was being nosy.

"Yeah." Laura paused. "I let him feel me up under my blouse . . . *over* my bra, of course," Laura added.

"No kidding!" Joss had never imagined Laura was so experienced.

Once in school Bobo had passed around a purity test that a friend of hers from camp had mailed to her. There were a million questions on it, and you got a point or two for every "yes" answer. Have you ever been kissed? . . . Kissed in the ear? . . . Kissed lying down? And so on. Joss' score was so pathetic she was in the absolute lowest category—"Ice Maiden." She hadn't even made it to the next step up, "Old-Fashioned Prude." But Laura, she bet, was at least in the "Live Wire" range and possibly even up to "Now You're Cookin'."

"What was it like when you did that?" Joss asked tentatively. She couldn't imagine it in a zillion years, someone groping all over her. How could you face each other afterward? It would be so embarrassing.

"I'm not really sure. I had some Kleenex stuffed in my bra, so I couldn't feel much of anything."

Joss burst out laughing. "Oh, Laura. *No!*"

Laura nodded dolefully. "I was so humiliated. You're lucky, Joss. That's something you'll never have to worry about."

"But I hate being big," Joss blurted out vehemently. "I'd much rather be flat like you. I feel like I stick out a mile, and I'm always worrying if my shirt is too tight."

"I should have such problems," Laura said. "Listen to this. One day last summer when my hair was very short, I was with a whole bunch of kids at a Bob's Big Boy, and the waitress looked at me and said, 'So what'll it be, sonny?' I nearly died."

Joss could feel her cheeks being pulled. "Ooh, Laur. Don't make me laugh. My face is starting to feel tight."

"Mine, too. I guess the mask must really be working." Laura rolled halfway over onto her side so that her gray-green face was staring directly into Joss'. "So? Aren't you going to tell me how far you've gone after I went and told you everything?"

"There's nothing to tell. I've never done anything— I mean zilch! Unless of course you count that lovely moment up in my attic with Fletcher . . . which I don't," Joss was quick to assure Laura.

"Oh boy," Laura moaned. "Now you probably think I'm really fast."

"I don't, Laur. I swear!" Joss exclaimed with fervor. "The only reason I've never done anything is because I've never had the chance. It's not like I think making out is bad. Honest."

"Well, I'd never do *anything* below the waist," Laura righteously proclaimed. "Not unless I knew it was really true love. And I don't plan on going all the way until I'm at least a sophomore in college. Maybe even older."

"It sounds so gross to me. Going all the way. I

don't even see how it can work," Joss mused, propping her now rock-hard chin on her hand. "Once when I had my period I tried using Tampax. But there was no way I could get it to go in. I think maybe there's something wrong with me . . . with the way I'm built."

"No, I thought the same thing. You just have to be relaxed." Laura sighed and clasped her dragonlady fingers behind her head. "I don't know. It does sound pretty weird, going all the way. But it must be great, or why would everybody do it?"

"I don't know. But I don't plan on finding out. Not for a long time." If ever, Joss added to herself.

Seven thirty.

Joss was in a state. The beauty mask hadn't worked. Her whole face felt chapped and raw, and even with all the Cover Girl base she'd smeared on it, Joss was sure her zits stood out more than ever, especially the beaut on her forehead, which was practically the size of a headlight.

Peering into the full-length mirror on the inside of Laura's closet, Joss took a piece of her bangs and tried plastering the hair over her forehead. There. Did that hide the zit? No! Plus her bangs looked all stringy and greasy. *Wunderbar*!

"Now you're absolutely sure my breath is okay?" Laura asked for the fiftieth time and began blowing into her cupped hands again, sniffing like a bloodhound.

"I keep telling you, it's fine. Fine. If everybody had breath like yours, Lavoris would be out of business."

"Yeah, yeah. Madame Fein's friends probably tell *her* that, too."

Joss laughed. Madame Fein's breath was a lethal weapon.

Laura squeezed next to Joss and surveyed their dual reflections. "Oh God!" she squealed with wide eyes. "Look!"

"What! What is it?" Joss fairly shrieked. What horrendous thing had she overlooked?

"We clash!" Laura wailed. "I never thought of that before. This red," Laura pointed down at her own dress, "looks grotesque next to the blue-green you're wearing."

"Is that all? You really had me scared," Joss said as she rubbed her nose to get some of the shine off it. "Lookit, hopefully we won't be together all night, and no one will notice. Right?"

"Right." Laura let out a high-pitched giggle and squeezed Joss' sweaty hand in hers. "I'm so nervous."

"*Moi aussi.*" Joss gave herself one final inspection in the mirror. At least the new dress looked decent, and the eye makeup, which had some glittery stuff in it, was truly glamorous. And the way her little gold studs winked through her hair. That looked nice, too. All right. So maybe she wasn't a total disaster. . . .

Laura smoothed her skirt, moistened her lips with her tongue—"That's supposed to look verrry sexy," she informed Joss—and then, looking at each other with a nod that said it was now or never, they marched out into the soft night air.

Bobo lived just two blocks down in the Colonial Heritage development, in a two-story white house with blue shutters. The door was wide open. Joss could hear music blasting from the basement.

Together Joss and Laura made their entrance. Several heads turned to see who the newest arrivals were. At that moment Joss couldn't help wishing she'd come with a fat friend, a real blimp, someone who would make her look positively anorectic.

Right away Laura made a beeline for Fletcher. He and a couple of other boys were tossing M&M's into the air and catching them in their mouths while a bunch of girls from their class were all squeezed together on one couch watching the performance. Everyone was dressed up except Fletcher, who had on jeans with a T-shirt painted to look like the front of a tuxedo.

"It's about time you got here." Fletcher had to yell to be heard over the music.

"I always arrive fashionably late," Laura screamed back. "Hey, Fletcher, I like your outfit. *Très* spiffy."

"K-Mart's finest," Fletcher shouted proudly. Was it Joss' imagination, or had he just flashed a tentative, conciliatory smile her way? Hard to tell with all the lights so dim.

Nervously Joss scanned the room. No sign of Bobo. Or Twig, for that matter. And then she saw a pair of old Topsiders come down the basement steps followed by faded khaki pants, a navy blue blazer and striped tie, and the smile. The Smile. Oh God! Twig looked gorgeous. Fletcher would probably say he looked "terminally preppy" or "wall-to-wall Wasp." But Joss thought he was absolutely perfect.

"Gangway!" Twig brushed past her with a teetering stack of record albums in his arms. "Oh, Joss! Hi!"

"Hi, Twig," Joss squeaked back. Her throat went dry, and she felt her upper lip stick to her gums as she tried to smile.

"Don't go away. I'll be back in a sec."

Joss nodded dumbly, trying as inconspicuously as possible to dislodge her lip with her tongue. "I've just got to unload these," Twig called over his shoulder.

"Oh, Twig. There you are." Bobo came charging down the basement steps two at a time. "Thanks a heap for bringing those records down for me. Just put them over here." Bobo pointed to a low Formica table. "Maybe you can help me pick out what to put on next."

Bobo was buzzing all around now like some killer bee, and adroitly wedging herself between Twig and Joss, she managed to steer him over to the stereo.

Joss caught the annoyed look that Laura was telegraphing her way. It said, "Don't just stand there. *Do* something." But Joss just shrugged her shoulders, feeling she was no match for Bobo, who was smiling and nodding at something Twig was saying. God, she made it look so easy, talking to a boy. She made it look like it was the most natural thing in the world. Joss gravitated to a mammoth bowl of Cheez Doodles and munched dejectedly while she spied on Bobo and Twig. There she went again, touching Twig on the arm. Now she was whispering something in his ear.

There was a moment of silence before the next album came on, and Bobo took a step into the middle of the room. "Okay, group," Bobo said, clapping her hands for attention. "Now lookit, you guys. I've seen wilder study halls than this. This is a party. Remember? So everybody start dancing. Okay?"

Some more Cheez Doodles found their way into Joss' mouth. She had to hand it to Bobo. Oozing confidence from every pore. Only Bobo could get away with a remark like that and somehow make it seem like it would be everybody else's fault, but not hers, if the party was a dud.

"Jocelyn Longman. This is my cousin, Tony Haver. He goes to Deerfield." Bobo practically shoved a blond, heavyset giant in front of Joss before she and Twig positioned themselves in the center of the room and began dancing.

"You in Bobo's class?" asked the cousin. He looked old, maybe even sixteen, with the scraggly beginnings of a mustache that he kept stroking.

"Ummm, yes." Joss was sneaking glances at Twig. Maybe he was only dancing with Bobo because she was the hostess. Still, he didn't exactly look like he was suffering.

"Want to dance?"

"What?"

"I said, 'Do—you—want—to—dance?' " The blond boy enunciated each word very slowly.

"Oh, sure. Sorry," Joss mumbled.

Scrunched in among a small but growing crowd of wildly bouncing bodies, Joss moved to the beat of the music. Nearby, Laura and Fletcher were flailing away with abandon. Since when had Fletcher learned to dance? Oh well, it was nice to see somebody was having fun. Joss tried her best not to look spastic. Who knew? Maybe Twig was watching her.

"Oops, sorry." Joss accidentally jabbed Tony in the stomach with her elbow.

"It's okay. I can take it. I play football at Deerfield."

When the next song, a long slow one, began, Tony pulled Joss to him, catching her off-balance so that she wound up with her face pressed against his chest, the buttons on his button-down collar digging into her cheek. She yanked herself away. Tony glanced down at her briefly with a look of mild surprise. Without even waiting for the song to end, he muttered something about wanting a Coke and left Joss at her original post next to the Cheez Doodles.

Now what? Joss thought, dipping into the bowl again. Here she was standing around like a lunk watching Bobo and Twig slow dance. Her worst fears come true!

Michelle came over and stood beside her.

"Hi, Michelle," Joss said. "You look nice."

"Thanks. So do you. Great party, huh?" Michelle

swayed back and forth to the music. "Oh, look at Bobo with Twig! They make a real cute couple, don't you think?"

"Mmmm. Adorable."

Richie Valente, the smartest kid in the class, came up to them. He was wearing a blue suit, and for once there wasn't a calculator sticking out of his pocket.

"C'mon, Michelle," he said, grabbing her hand, and dragged her off to dance.

On and on the music played. Joss' hand groped for more Cheez Doodles, and when she looked down into the bowl, she was horrified to see it was almost empty. And her hands! They were covered with bright orange Cheez Doodle dust.

Joss headed for the bathroom.

"Hi!"

She spun around. It was Twig. Somehow he'd gotten free of Bobo.

"What happened to your friend?" Twig asked.

Joss looked at Twig blankly.

"The tall blond kid. Bobo's cousin."

So Twig *had* noticed. "Oh, him." Joss tried to sound as if so many boys were beating down her door that it was hard to keep track of them all.

"You look really nice, Jocelyn."

"Thanks. So do you." Did it sound really retarded to say that to a boy?

"So. You want to dance?"

"Sure."

It was another slow song. Joss took the hand Twig

held out to her and prayed she wouldn't get Cheez Doodle dust all over him. They began to move in small, stiff circles about the crowded basement floor. Joss felt as wooden as a department store dummy. Relax, she commanded herself. But her body—all two tons of it—refused to obey.

At one point Joss' and Laura's eyes met. She was draped over Fletcher's shoulder so that it almost appeared as if he were dragging her around rather than dancing with her. Laura winked elaborately and made motions for Joss to move closer to Twig.

"Will you *stop* that?" Joss hissed the words to her.

"Did you say something?"

"No, no, Twig," Joss burbled. "I was just singing along with the record. I really like this song a lot." It was an old Blondie hit.

"Yeah? Me, too. I always thought Blondie was a great group."

"No kidding. Me, too! I love Deborah Harry. Her voice is so great." From the corner of her eye Joss could see Michelle and Bobo coming down the stairs, armed with fresh supplies of pretzels and Cheez Doodles. Joss' heart sank. In a minute, probably as soon as this song ended, Twig would be back at Bobo's side.

"Hey, Joss. It's awfully hot in here," Twig suddenly whispered to her. "Let's go someplace where it's less crowded. Okay?"

What! Twig wanted to be with her. Alone!

Overcome, Joss let him take her hand and lead her

through a door into the part of the basement where the furnace was. It was dark and hot, and Joss nearly tripped over an upended ironing board.

Twig started dancing with her again. Much closer this time. Outside, Joss could hear Bobo asking, "Has anybody seen Twig? Where is he? I want him to pick out the next song."

Joss half expected Twig to go rushing out when he heard his name called. But instead he whispered conspiratorially, "Bobo. She's too much." The way he said it did not seem like a compliment. "She's going to turn out just like my mother. I can tell. Always has to be in *charge* of everything." Twig paused for a moment. "You don't seem so sure of yourself. I think that's nice."

Joss was thrilled. It had never occurred to her that anyone, least of all Twig, might like her for what she considered her shortcomings.

"Plus you have terrific eyes."

If I die now, Joss thought, I die happy.

"I think green eyes are beautiful."

Actually her eyes were more a yellowy hazel color, but who was arguing?

Suddenly Twig was holding her tighter. They were so close now that his breath thrummed against the side of her neck in hot little gusts. It tickled, but Joss bit down on the inside of her mouth so she wouldn't laugh. She tried to copy the way she'd seen Laura dancing with Fletcher before. She transferred her left hand from Twig's shoulder to his collar so that her fingertips just barely grazed his neck. Then she rested her head on his shoulder. That was a little difficult since they were practically the same height. But Joss hunched down a little, and it seemed to work out all right.

"So you really like music, huh?" Twig said. His voice was hoarse and low.

"Uh-huh."

"Duran Duran is supposed to give a concert at the Springfield Auditorium sometime in June. I'm going to get tickets. If you want, I could get one for you, too."

"Sure. That'd be super," Joss said into Twig's chest. What did this mean? Had Twig just asked her out on a date? Maybe so, because now Twig was pulling her back away from him slightly. He smiled, and Joss thought wildly, Oh God! Here it comes. He's going to kiss me.

She squeezed her eyes shut and tried to keep her mouth slightly open and her lips parted. That was the way they always did it in the movies. Then why did she feel like she was at the dentist's?

The kiss went on much longer than she expected. Joss opened her eyes. This close up, Twig looked like a Cyclops.

At last he came up for air.

"Hey, Joss. What's the matter? You seem like you're on another planet."

"Nothing's the matter, Twig. Really." Joss tried moistening her lips the sexy way Laura had demonstrated. But her mouth felt all funny and out of shape. Like it was made of rubber.

"Don't you want to kiss me? Don't you like me even a little?"

Was he serious? "Believe me, Twig. I like you a lot more than a little," Joss said. "Come on. Let's try it again."

"Eleven times! Twig kissed me eleven times," Joss repeated rapturously in the dark of Laura's room. "A couple of them I bet lasted at least thirty seconds."

"Fletcher kissed me twice." Laura's disembodied voice came floating over from the other bed. "Right at the end of the party. The first time he sort of missed and got me on the nose." Laura giggled. "But it's the thought that counts, right?"

"I'm happy it all worked out like you wanted, Laur," Joss replied. And this time she wasn't just faking it. She really did mean it. She felt happy for Fletcher, too. If only there was some way to tell him that.

"Now if you and Fletcher were friends again, everything would be perfect." Laura sat up in bed. Joss could make out her silhouette against the window. "Just think how neat it'd be if we all could go on double dates together. You, me, Twig, and Fletcher."

"Yeah," Joss' voice trailed off. Tonight had been a true milestone. For the first time in her life she'd made out. Eleven kisses had to count as making out. She was almost sure of that. Joss sat up now, clasping her knees. "Laur, it was so terrific! I mean, I didn't hear violins or anything. But still. It was wonderful."

"Too bad you couldn't see Bobo's face when she realized you and Twig had disappeared. She ended up making out with some boy from Deerfield. A friend of her cousin's. But you could tell her heart wasn't in it."

"That's what I still can't understand, how Twig would want to be with me instead of her."

"Gee, Jocelyn. You really have a high opinion of yourself. Did you ever stop to think that you're ten times nicer and *lots* more fun?"

"But she's so cute. Cute counts for a lot."

"She's completely stuck on herself. Twig knows it. Besides, I love your looks. You've got an interesting face."

"Really? You think so?" It was the same thing Mom had said a hundred times. Somehow it sounded much better coming from Laura. Joss lay back and pulled the covers up over her. I am interesting looking, she repeated to herself. And Twig thinks I have pretty eyes. No. *Terrific* eyes. That's what he said. Snuggling under Laura's satiny bedspread, Joss tried to recapture what it had been like kissing him. There had been a whooshy sensation in the pit of her stomach. She remembered that. And a feeling of being off balance, like going down a step you didn't know was there. Only much nicer, of course.

"Hey, Laur," Joss whispered, eager to talk more. But Laura, already half asleep, only mumbled a groggy "Night."

Under her shortie pajamas, Joss ran her hand lightly over her breasts and down to her belly. Soft and round. That's how she felt. She tried pretending it was Twig's hand touching her.

Maybe next time I will go even farther with Twig, Joss conceded to herself. Maybe next time she would try French kissing. It sounded gross, having someone's slimy tongue in your mouth, but who knew. It might be worth a try. In any event, Joss hoped, yes, she fervently, desperately, wholeheartedly hoped that there would be a next time.

Ten

Joss barged through the door of her house, flung down her books on the front hall table, and darted up the stairs for the bathroom two at a time. In history, while Mr. Werner was droning on about the Lincoln-Douglas debates, her left ear had begun to itch. That was the first sign of infection, according to Sharon's warning list, and sure enough, when Joss had examined both ears in the girls' room right before lunch, her left one was redder.

Now Joss bolted down the hall to the bathroom for the tube of ointment she'd bought for just such an emergency. As she swung open the door of the medicine cabinet, the mirror reflected into her parents' room.

She was not alone.

There, on the faded flower-print chaise by the window, were Mom and Daddy, sitting together quietly, framed within the bathroom mirror. Daddy was hovering over Mom, his arm around her, while she was crying quietly and holding on to something in her hand.

Oh God! It was happening. It was really happening. Joss could not pull her eyes away from the mirror. Somehow she had expected a noisy, dramatic ending. Not this eerily calm scene.

It was Daddy who saw her first. He nudged her mother, who quickly wiped her eyes with the back of her hand.

"Come on in, Joss. Don't just stand there," Daddy finally said in a falsely hearty voice. "You're part of this occasion, too."

Occasion! That's what Daddy thought it was! Joss felt as if she were grafted to the floor of the bathroom, roots growing out from the soles of her feet. Somehow she wound up in her parents' room, facing the two of them.

"Aren't you going to say anything?" That was from Daddy.

Say what? Joss wondered. What could she possibly say?

Daddy sighed in a good-natured way. "Really, Ducks, you might stop looking like something out of *Night of the Living Dead* and wish us a happy anniversary!"

Anniversary! What was going on? Joss' brain felt blocked. She just continued to stare, fixing her gaze first on Daddy, then on Mom, who was red-eyed but smiling. Mom clicked open the small gray box she held in her hand. The white satiny inside, Joss could see, was stamped "DEWITT BROS., Fine Jewelers." "Come look at what Daddy gave me, honey."

It was a thin bar pin of delicate, lacy gold with a smooth deep blue stone in the center. It looked very old and very beautiful.

An anniversary present. You didn't give an anniversary present to someone you wanted to divorce.

"I'm sorry," Joss finally choked out. "I forgot all about it. Happy anniversary."

"It's perfect, isn't it?" Mom said, sniffing.

Daddy looked pleased. "I have to confess I got help. I couldn't decide between this and one other, but I happened to run into Phoebe Jackson downtown, so she took a look at both of them and convinced me this was it."

So that was what Phoebe and Daddy had been doing together that day she saw them. Picking out an anniversary present for Mom. Nothing more.

"I know I haven't been any prize to live with lately," Daddy went on. "Maybe not even just lately." He rubbed the stubble on his cheek in a slow, tired way. "I've let stupid things—work things—get to me too much. I know that. I need to pay more attention to the things that really count." He touched Mom lightly on the face, brushing back a strand of hair, and tears began trickling down her cheeks again. "Of course, when I thought about giving your mother her present, I pictured a somewhat different reaction." Daddy looked embarrassed.

"It's just that this is so sweet. So incredibly sweet." Mom sounded like she was trying to make excuses for herself.

As far as Joss was concerned, it seemed entirely natural for Mom to be bawling away. She was obviously crying from relief after all that worrying over Daddy. Joss felt like crying too, especially when her eye caught the small white card lying next to the crumpled-up wrapping paper on the chaise. "Stay with me forever . . . wherever."

Joss woke up, sun slanting in through her window, splashing giant polka dots of light against her wall. For a minute she couldn't remember why she felt so happy. Then it hit her. Yesterday. Mom and Daddy.

Joss lay back in bed and tried to piece together the reasons she'd been so convinced Daddy had been in love with Phoebe Jackson. Let's see. There was the time she came upon them at Daddy's office. And all the times Phoebe'd called or dropped by unexpectedly at the house. And of course the fateful day at Dewitt's. Now everything that had added together to signal something so horrible and unavoidable suddenly seemed to shrink into nothing at all. Could the whole "affair" really have been all in her mind? It was frightening to think she could have made up something like that.

Joss stretched and peered at her clock. Seven forty. Astounded, she held it to her ear to make sure it was ticking. Normally she never stumbled out of bed before noon on weekends, bleary eyed and heavy lidded. But this morning she was itching to get dressed and get out.

Humming, Joss went to the window. The sky that poked through the latticework of branches was an unreal, Crayola blue, like in the postcards of Higham sold in the souvenir shops downtown.

> "Ta-da da da dum,
> Lift up your head and shout
> It's gonna be a great day,"

Joss sang while she fished out a pair of jeans and a clean polo shirt from her dresser. A moment later she was tiptoeing past her parents' room. Lord only knew what time they'd come in last night. Dad had insisted on taking Mom to the Stiles Inn for a long, quiet dinner. Just the two of them.

While she taped a note to the toaster that said, "Gone for the day—J," Joss tried to figure out exactly how long it had been since her parents had gone any place alone together. Two months? Four months? Ages, anyway.

Outside, Joss wheeled her bike down the gravel driveway to the street. She hopped on and began coasting down the hill toward the main street of town, her hair whipping across her face as she built up speed.

Happily Joss pedaled on through the heart of downtown—all three streets of it—not exactly sure just where it was she was heading. Laura was away for the weekend. In Boston with her father. Anyway, Laura was the last person Joss could imagine wanting to go on a long bike ride. Applying eyeliner was about the most strenuous exercise Laura got voluntarily.

She could head out to Twig's house and maybe see him "by accident." No, that would be too obvious, and anyway, why bother with tricks like that when they had an official date next weekend!

At the corner of Main and Trumbull, Joss decided to stop for breakfast at Kramer's Fountain. It was one of the few places that was open this early.

Whenever she went to the doctor, Mom always took her to Kramer's afterward for coffee milk shakes as a treat. And today Joss felt like treating herself.

Inside, Mr. Kramer was wiping off the counter. A radio was playing, and a heavyset man opposite him was smoking a cigarette, flicking ashes into the saucer of his coffee cup.

Joss perched herself on one of the patched, red leather stools. Once Fletcher had spun himself around on one so fast that the seat had finally come flying off, and he'd gone crashing into a display rack of panty hose.

"So what'll it be, kid?" Mr. Kramer made a point of never knowing anybody's name.

"An English muffin and . . . a coffee shake," Joss added impulsively.

"A little early to be hitting the sauce, isn't it?"

"Today's a special occasion." Joss didn't know exactly why she said that. But it seemed true. She picked up one of the magazines from the stack that was always kept on the counter for customers. It was an old issue of People magazine with J. R. Ewing from *Dallas* on the cover. "The Guy You Love to Hate," it said. Joss flipped through the inside while Mr. Kramer popped down the toaster and began pouring milk and syrup and ice cream into a tall silver cup.

"Hey! It's seventy-four degrees at eight thirty," a peppy radio announcer informed them. *"The magic W-A-N-D weatherman calls for clear skies with temperatures climbing into the eighties. And now here's one you'll remember from Tony Orlando and Dawn. . . ."*

"Gonna be another hot one." The heavyset man rubbed out his cigarette and pushed some change across the counter before squeezing himself off the stool.

"Be seeing you, buddy." The whir of the blender stopped, and Mr. Kramer poured the foaming liquid from the silver container into a glass and passed them both to Joss. A moment later the muffin arrived, a pat of melting butter dribbling off it onto the plate.

While she leisurely sipped and munched, Joss read an article in *People* called "Where Are They Now?" It was about people who had once been famous. A

174

former Mouseketeer from the *Mickey Mouse Club* show was photographed combing out some woman's hair at the beauty parlor where she worked. An injured football player posed in front of the barbecue restaurant he had just opened. "Pig out at the Pigskin Palace," it said in neon letters above him. And an ex-politician who'd just come out of jail said he was "presently campaigning full-time for our Lord, Jesus Christ."

Joss felt sorriest for the Mouseketeer/beautician. "I was never that big on talent, mind you," the article quoted her as saying. "But was I ever cute with my curls and my dimples and my little mouse ears! Then I got older and I guess I just wasn't that cute anymore. Anyway, Disney dropped me from the show. It really messed me up for a while. I ran away from home at fifteen, and the rest, as they say, is history."

The football player had gotten a raw deal too. "One minute I'm hauling my butt down the field for a touchdown and I'm thinking 'Hello, Superbowl.' The next thing I know I get blindsided by some dumb linebacker, and when I wake up from the anesthesia I've got two steel kneecaps."

Joss poured the remainder of the milk shake from the silver container into her glass. It certainly was weird, how life could pull a fast one on you. Without any warning.

That made her think of a passage from Millie's diary, one of the very last entries. Joss remembered

Millie writing, after Elliot's death, "I feel as if my life, too, has been blown to bits."

Joss shut the magazine. Millie was just like those people in the article. Everything rolling along just swell and then—ZAP! What must it have been like for Millie, knowing the future was never going to turn out the way she had planned it? It was strange, Joss supposed, knowing so much about Millie's life up until Elliot died and then knowing almost nothing after that. What had happened to Millie during all those years alone?

Suddenly Joss knew what she was going to do today. Loudly, she sucked up the last of the milk shake through her straw, thanked Mr. Kramer as she paid, and hurried past the rows of cosmetics and deodorants and baby products to the old wood phone booth in back.

Inside, a beat-up directory for Deerfield and Higham hung from a string with a big chunk of the middle section torn out, but the page Joss needed was still there.

She sat down and dialed. On the fourth ring, Mrs. Trilling picked up.

"Of course I remember you," she said. "It isn't likely I'd forget a fellow snoop!"

A few moments later Joss was pedaling down Route 4 heading toward Deerfield, trying to keep the directions straight in her head. When I get to the center of town, take the first right at the traffic light by the A&P and go straight until I hit Winwood, then just hang a left and keep going to the end of the road. . . . Mrs. Trilling had said she'd be waiting outside.

As she pedaled into Deerfield, Joss pictured a twin of her own house or at least something very close to it. Instead she found herself approaching a white brick building, several stories high. A sign announcing "Sunset Village" was planted in the yard out front, and several old ladies and a few old men were sitting on benches, their faces turned toward the sun.

A nursing home!

One of the old ladies was coming toward her, and it took a second for Joss to see that it was Mrs. Trilling herself.

"Welcome to Senile City!" she called out to Joss.

Joss waved. "Hello, Mrs. Trilling."

"Why don't you forget the Mrs. Trilling. Weezie will do just fine. That's how you know me, after all. And it'd be nice to have somebody calling me that again."

"All right . . . Weezie." Joss tried it out tentatively and found it wasn't half so bad as when Fletcher's father had started insisting on Mortimer instead of Dr. Dwoskin.

Weezie led her up the concrete path to the main building. In the bright light Joss could see she had put on way too much face powder, some of which was all over the front of her dress.

"This is the main house," Weezie explained. "They try to run it like a hotel. Everybody has a private room. Bath. Maid service. You can come and go pretty much as you please. That is, as long as you've got most of your marbles." Weezie tapped her forehead for emphasis. "The bad ones are moved to the infirmary." She pointed to a low structure to their left. "Sooner or later everybody lands up there unless you're fortunate enough to check out suddenly."

Joss tried to imagine herself with wrinkles and gnarled hands, walking with a stoop. It was impossible. Mom once said that if she didn't look in the mirror, she'd never believe she was thirty-three. Inside she still felt young. Was it the same way for Weezie?

"It was because of Mill that I came here," Weezie went on. "One night I kept calling and calling but there was no answer at her house. Since it was late, I phoned the police. They found her on the kitchen floor. Had a stroke. Couldn't even get to the phone."

"God, that's horrible." Joss shuddered. "Had she been there long? Was she still alive?"

"Just barely. Died a couple of days later." Weezie sighed. "Poor Millie. Anyway, I said to myself, 'Louisa Trilling, that is *not* for you.' So I signed myself in here. God's Waiting Room we call it."

Joss wheeled her bike up the ramp for wheelchairs to the front entrance. The doors whooshed apart automatically, like at airports, and she and Weezie entered a lobby with bright orange carpeting and lots of fake plants. How could Weezie be so matter-of-fact, so practical about dying, Joss wondered, as she maneuvered her bike into the elevator. Was it possible to believe, really and truly believe, that it was going to happen to you?

"Well, here we are. Room Sweet Room," Weezie was saying, turning her key and opening the door. "Better leave that bike out here. We'll need a shoehorn just to fit the both of us inside."

No lie, Joss thought a second later. The room was tiny. A bed with a gray metal frame took up most of the space. There was a pot of African violets on the windowsill, a few framed photographs on the dresser, and a blue and yellow Afghan thrown over the back of an armchair.

"I suppose you're ready for our stroll down memory lane." Weezie motioned for Joss to sit down on the bed. There was a shoebox on it marked "Blk Pat 6 1/2N." Weezie moved the chair next to the bed, sat down, and began sifting through the contents. "Let's start in the Pleistocene Era, shall we, when Clara and Mill and I were children."

"You mean they *had* photographs then?" Joss asked in mock surprise.

"Fresh kid," Weezie muttered with a smile, while she handed over several snapshots.

The pictures were old indeed. If the faded brown tints weren't proof enough, there were dates, neatly written on the back of each snapshot. "Grandfather Trilling, 1898" . . . "The family in Chilicote, Maine, 1903" . . . "Clara with Baby Louisa, 1906."

"Look at you here. This one is *wonderful*." Joss pointed to a picture of Weezie, who looked to be about four or five. She was wearing an unwieldy wide-brimmed hat, high button shoes, a coat with an elaborate fur collar, and an exceedingly belligerent expression.

Weezie snorted. "Imagine. Dressing children like that. Ridiculous. Utterly ridiculous. I remember the day that picture was taken. The only governess I ever liked, and the only one who ever liked me, had just been sacked after Mother found a pack of cigarettes in her room."

"Fired? Just for that?"

"Nice girls—ladies—didn't smoke."

"But that's so dumb."

"There was a lot 'dumb' in those days. But weren't you the girl who wanted to grow up then? Because you like rules so much."

Joss flushed. Weezie had a good memory. "I don't know. I *think* I would've liked living back then, but who knows. Maybe I would have fought all the rules, too. Hey, look." Joss pushed back her hair and pointed to her ears. "I got 'em pierced last week . . . without my mother's permission."

"An act of open rebellion. What will come next?"

"Make fun if you want, but this was big time for me." Joss stopped. The photo she had just turned over said "Millicent M. and Clara, summer, 1910."

"Well, I finally get to see Millie."

Weezie bent closer to Joss. "That's Mill on the left," she said.

"I know." Joss was sure she could have picked her

out of any crowd. Throughout her diary Millie was always lamenting her looks, calling herself a "clod," declaring she was "as plain as a spud potato." Now Joss had to admit that Millie was right. It would have been wrong to call her ugly. Millie was too undistinguished-looking for that. But she *was* plain, with her round moon of a face and wide fat cheeks. Perched on a rock in her prim high-collared blouse, Millie reminded Joss of a bird. Not in the frail, sparrow-like sense. More like a pigeon or a hen. Plump and squat. Even the way she sat, with her knees drawn in under her long dark skirt, made it seem as if she was roosting.

"I wonder if it was tough on Millie having a best friend as beautiful as Clara," Joss mused out loud. "She never says anything like that in her diary. But still . . ."

Weezie shook her head. "Mill wasn't that way. Spiteful or mean. No. *I* was the one who was jealous of Clara. Jealous, too, of her friendship with Mill, I suppose." Weezie leaned back in her chair. She was looking in Joss' direction but without really focusing on her. "Lordy, they were inseparable. Clara was always a very sweet, biddable girl. Mill had more of the devil in her. Smarter, too. She could talk Clara into almost anything." Weezie laughed to herself. "One time they went around the neighborhood collecting money for 'poor orphans.' Of course, *they* were the poor orphans, and when Mother found out . . . well, in those days nobody thought twice about giving a child a good licking." Weezie leaned forward and watched as Joss shuffled through more photos. "Ah, look. There they are at Miss Nesbitt's. Millie was a good student. Did you know she went on to Bronwyn?"

"That's where my father teaches! No, I didn't know she'd gone there. I really don't know anything much that happened to Millie after Elliot was killed except that she never got married."

"Then you do have some catching up to do, don't you?" Weezie hoisted herself out of the chair and burrowed around in the top drawer of her bureau. "Here." She handed Joss a couple of graham crackers and kept a few for herself. "Strictly against house rules to keep food in your room. Bugs, and all. But I figure you won't squeal on an old lady."

Joss giggled. "My lips are sealed."

Weezie rearranged herself in her chair again. "Now where was I? Oh, Bronwyn. Yes! Well, Mill's father wouldn't hear of it at first. Wanted her to go to some posh finishing school instead. Thought it 'unseemly' for a girl to be too educated. Then when he found out one of the Lorimer girls was going to Bronwyn, he relented."

"That sounds like Phineas," Joss said. "I don't think I could have stood it, having him for a father. He sounds like such a bully. I always picture him big and fat with a huge drooping mustache. Like a walrus."

"Well, he *was* a large man but, sorry, no mustache.

Phineas' problem was that he made his money—lots of it, my dear—fairly late in life. The older established families—the Lorimers and the Harpers—never truly accepted him and he knew it. Oh, how it ate at him. Always worrying about 'doing the right thing'; I never knew a man before or since who put so much store in being 'refined.' He nearly died himself after the mayor choked at his house. It drove him crazy the way all the folks in town joked about it."

"You know, Phineas is still up in our attic. His ashes, I mean."

Weezie hooted and slapped her knee. "Is that a fact? Of course, I shouldn't laugh. But I can just imagine what old Phineas would think of his final resting place."

"When I was little, I used to think that if I rubbed the urn, he would pop out. Like a genie. I was scared stiff to even go near it." Joss rifled through the box. "I think Millie was scared of him, too. . . . Well, maybe not scared exactly. But she was always worrying what he thought of her. She was scared that he didn't like Elliot." Joss sifted through more pictures. "Are there any in here of Elliot? Or of Millie and Elliot together?"

"I did have a few." Weezie took the box from Joss and shuffled down deeper in it. "But damned if I can find any. . . . Oh, now here's one from Jack and Clara's wedding. But it's not very good." Weezie passed the photo to Joss, who examined it eagerly.

The bride and groom were flanked by several men in top hats and several bridesmaids holding large bouquets.

Joss spotted Millie right beside Clara, and the flower girl in front, she realized, had to be Weezie. Still looking belligerent.

"Elliot's the one on the very end," Weezie said.

"Rats!" Joss muttered. "Why'd he have to be looking down? You can't really see his face at all." Then Joss noticed the date of the picture. "Why, this was taken only a month before he died!"

"Yes, all the fellows we knew were sent at the same time. But Elliot was the only one who didn't make it back."

"Poor Elliot! Poor Millie. She looks so happy here. And it was all going to end so soon." Joss gazed at the doomed lovers as she started on her second cracker. At least it had been perfect while it lasted. That had to have been some comfort to Millie all those lonely years.

"Poor Elliot is right. He had no business signing up. If not for Mill, he wouldn't have."

"What do you mean, 'if not for Mill'?" Joss asked, surprised.

Weezie looked surprised, too. "Didn't Millie write about that in her diary?"

"Write what? What are you talking about?"

Now Weezie seemed reluctant to go on.

"Please. Oh, please tell me," Joss said.

"Well, Elliot had always been frail. He lied his way

into the army. They never would have taken him otherwise. And he did it because of Mill."

"But that can't be right," Joss said, confused. "Why would Millie have wanted him to risk his life?"

"She didn't want to have the only beau who wasn't a soldier. I don't think she ever came out and said as much to Elliot or asked him to join up. But then, she wouldn't have had to."

Joss said nothing for a moment, looking down at the picture of Elliot at the wedding. "I don't understand. How could she do that to someone she loved?"

"Oh, you mustn't be too harsh on poor Mill. She was so young. I'm sure she never once considered that Elliot might die." Weezie sighed. "It's probably awful to say, but Elliot was just the type to go and get himself shot right away. He was a—what's the word I'm looking for?" Weezie clucked her tongue impatiently. "Nerd! That's it. Elliot was quite a nerd."

Nerd? The Elliot Joss had always pictured was sensitive, thoughtful. And above all, romantic.

"But Millie *loved* Elliot. He was her one true love," Joss insisted. "She's always saying how kind and wonderful he was in her diary. And after he died, she wrote that for her there would never be another."

Weezie looked apologetic. "I'm not saying Mill wasn't *fond* of Elliot. I'm not saying she didn't *like* him. But love . . .? You must remember she wasn't more than sixteen or seventeen at the time. Elliot was the first man who ever paid any attention to her. But he wasn't the last."

Joss studied Weezie for a moment. She was positive that she was going to like her own version of the Millie-Elliot story a thousand times better. Still, she found herself asking, "You mean she met somebody *else*?"

Weezie played with the gold wedding band on her finger. "A few years after college Mill went to Boston. Taught history in a public school there. A public school! You can imagine what Phineas thought of that! Anyway, Mill met another teacher. A widower almost her father's age. They never did get married, but from what she told me, they were happy together. After he died, she moved back to Higham. That's when we became friends."

Joss stared out the window and tried to take in what Weezie had just told her. "I pictured it so differently. All this time I was imagining Romeo and Juliet right here in Higham."

Joss thought again of the day she'd seen Daddy with Phoebe Jackson at the jewelry store. A long, low sigh escaped her. It was all so confusing. How could you ever know for certain what was real? It was like those stupid pictures in the psychology book that Fletcher had shown her. You could never be sure what you were seeing. The lady or the skull.

"You must think I'm really dumb," she finally said to Weezie. "Building this whole thing up in my mind." Weezie shook her head and started to speak, but Joss went on. "All this time I thought Millie was treasuring

Elliot's memory, when she was actually living with some other guy."

"First of all, I didn't say she lived with that man," Weezie replied.

"I just assumed when you said—"

"Oh, I find that's always a risky business. Assuming too much," Weezie said with a brisk shake of her head. "To be perfectly honest, I don't know what Mill's exact arrangement was with him. I'm not even sure he was her lover. She never said. People can have many different kinds of attachments, you know. And they don't always fall into neat categories."

Joss nodded, although personally she preferred to think of relationships as being clearly and boldly emblazoned. True love . . . best friend . . . devoted parent . . . What was so wrong with that?

She and Weezie got up at the same time. They both sensed the visit was over.

"I'll come again, some other time. That's if you want me to."

"Will you?" Weezie sounded as if she thought Joss was just being polite. "I'd like that very much."

As she showed Joss to the door, Weezie pressed another graham cracker into her hand. "One for the road," she said brightly, and closed the door.

Eleven

The ride back to Higham was torture. At the edge of town, halfway up the hill by Druids Lane cemetery, Joss finally gave up, got off her bike, and pushed it to the top. Now what? she wondered grumpily. It was still at least a mile or a mile and a half to her house, with another killer hill once she reached the college.

Resting her bike against the gentle incline that led up to the graveyard, Joss flopped down on the grass. Her visit with Weezie had left her feeling not depressed exactly, but dispirited. She should have known the real-life Millie and Elliot couldn't possibly live up to her image of them. Wearily Joss wiped her forehead with the bottom of her T-shirt.

Across the street was a row of large spooky Victorian houses that had been split up a few years ago into apartments for Bronwyn faculty. For a moment Joss considered ringing somebody's doorbell and calling home to see if Mom or Daddy could come pick her up. Instead she climbed the rise to the graveyard.

When they'd first moved to Higham, she and her mother had made a couple of pilgrimages out here to try their hand at some grave rubbing. One time Fletcher had come along too, but he'd acted like a complete cretin, tapping on the tombstones and calling, "Anybody home?" in a low, ghostly wail. Anyway, if she remembered correctly, there was a small terraced rock fountain close by, not the kind you could drink from, but at least she'd be able to splash some water on her face.

She found the fountain under a yew tree, but it gave forth such a meager trickle that Joss was barely able to wet her hands. Still, it was so nice and peaceful here—all she could hear was the distant buzzing of a lawn mower—and Joss paused for a moment to look at the soft, weathered gray slabs that surrounded her.

Some were so worn down and covered with moss that even in broad daylight you couldn't make out the names, while others, beaten down by hundreds of years of storms, stuck out of the ground at crazy angles, like crooked teeth. There were tons of Lorimers out here—it was a regular family reunion—but no Mortimers. After what Weezie had told her, it made Joss wonder whether Phineas had decided to go and

189

have himself cremated because he couldn't be buried with this select group.

Now, where was that tombstone that had always been Mom's favorite? Squatting down, Joss scanned the names as if she were going through a phone directory. Asa Forster! There he was. Marked with a crude skull, Asa Forster's tombstone issued the stern warning: "As ye are now, so once was I. Repent now, sinner. Ye soon shall die." Personally Joss preferred the gentler memorials to "good wyves" and "faithfull husbands" and the funny, awkward faces of angels that hovered at the tops of some of the stones. With their round staring eyes and silly pursed mouths, they looked like they were about to sneeze or had just smelled something awful. Joss had done a rubbing of one. It still hung in Daddy's study; Mom called it "Charlie's Angel."

Suddenly Joss heard a car screech out from the garage of one of the houses across the street. She looked up. Mom's car! It had to be. There couldn't be another pale-blue VW convertible in Higham that still had an "Impeach Nixon" bumper sticker on it.

Joss hurried down the hill ready to call out—now she could get a lift home. But Mom gunned the motor and flew off down the street as if she were making a getaway.

Weird, Joss thought, watching the car vanish down the road. She had expected her mother to be home. Who could she have been visiting, anyway? Joss couldn't think of anyone they knew who lived way

190

out here. Well, she'd have to ask when she got home.

Joss stared at her bike. The muscles in her legs were already cramping up, as if in protest. "Courage," she told herself and hopped on.

The sight of her mother's car parked in the driveway irritated Joss as she pedaled the last seemingly endless block to their house. Talk about pooped! Joss was sure she must have sweated off thirty pounds today. She'd have to weigh herself later. But first something cold to drink and then a long soak in the tub. "Phew." Joss caught a whiff of herself. If Twig could get a load of her now. Charming!

Joss hauled herself up the front steps. "*Je suis arrivée*," she croaked. "And you'll never guess who I just saw. Y-O-U!"

There was no reply from Mom. Then Joss heard her voice coming from upstairs. She was talking on the phone.

In the kitchen Joss grabbed for a glass and started to pull open the refrigerator door. It was then that she noticed the note. It was held in place on the refrigerator by a magnet in the shape of a tiny Popsicle. "Fletcher called. Asked you to please call him later. Sounded serious!?!" The message was scrawled in Daddy's childlike handwriting.

A whoop of pleasure and triumph escaped from Joss. Fletcher wanted to make up. He wanted to be friends again! That had to be why he had called. Talk about a switch. Should she wait and let him sweat it out for a while; let him worry whether *she* wanted to patch things up? No, that'd be rubbing it in too much, Joss concluded. It must have been hard for Fletcher to make the call—it was an all-time first, that was for sure. Joss figured she could afford to be generous.

Without thinking, Joss grabbed for the kitchen phone. As she placed the receiver to her ear, she caught a snatch of conversation.

"No." Her mother's voice was low and insistent. "I meant what I said."

"Oops, sorry," Joss was on the verge of saying before the voice at the other end stopped her cold.

"But you can't just say good-bye like that." A clipped British accent. Professor Macdunna.

"I can. I have to." Mom sounded firm but miserable. "I should never have gone over to your house in the first place. But I didn't know how else to end this. . . . I am not exactly an expert in these matters."

I am not hearing this. . . . I am not hearing this, Joss chanted to herself.

"Dorothy, please. You must know that I love—"

Joss banged down the phone. "Oh, no!" she heard her mother cry from above. There was a clattering down the stairs. Joss bolted for the door.

"Please, Joss, wait!" Mom was shouting.

Joss didn't. The door slammed behind her and she was gone.

How long had she been here on the island? Fifteen minutes? Two hours? It was hard to tell since, incredibly, Joss had fallen asleep. She remembered Fletcher once telling her about one of his father's patients who couldn't stay awake when anything really upsetting happened. The girl had finally flunked out of Bronwyn after her boyfriend broke up with her and she'd slept through all her final exams. It wasn't a bad solution, Joss reflected now, dislodging a sharp pebble that was jabbing into her side. The only drawback was having to wake up.

When Joss had raced out of the house, Mom had not tried to follow. Joss knew she wouldn't, yet she didn't stop running until she hit the Buster Keaton Playhouse by the college. She ducked inside. Some arty Italian movie, in black and white with subtitles, was playing. Blessedly there was still almost three dollars left in her pocket after the price of admission, so Joss put away a hot dog, two bags of M&M's, a box of Jujubes, and an extra-large popcorn soaked in rancid butter while she sat through the picture two times, crying and eating, eating and crying.

How perfectly thickheaded she'd been. It was Mom all along. Daddy's moodiness, his resentment of Mom spending so much time "studying." All of it was because he was scared *he* was losing *her*. And Mom's admiration for the professor, the crying spells, were because she was . . . Joss couldn't bear to say it. Not even to herself. All the signs had been there. Right

193

before her eyes. But she had read each and every one of them entirely the wrong way. Again she thought of those pictures Fletcher had shown her. She'd seen only what she wanted to see.

When she finally emerged from the theater, her eyes were red from crying and her whole face felt raw and sore. Joss wished she was a mole so she could tunnel underground.

Going to the island was the closest she could come. When she paddled across in the last canoe left in the boathouse, several girls from Bronwyn were also there. Some had books open, studying. Some were sailing Frisbees back and forth, and others were simply lounging around, taking in the last of the afternoon sun. But one by one they'd all gone.

Joss sat up now picking leaves out of her hair. The sky had deepened to a rich violet. Soon it would be dark. That had to mean it was around seven thirty. Mom would be growing anxious that she hadn't come home. Good! Joss hoped Mom was getting frantic. Let her think Joss had been picked up by a stranger in a car who had murdered her and thrown her mangled body in a heap on some deserted road. It would be on her mother's head forever! Joss tried to picture the scene at home right now. What excuse would Mom give to Daddy? Would she have to confess? Or did Daddy know already?

Without warning Joss began crying again. What a mess. She was not supposed to know what she knew. She was only thirteen. She wanted to bury herself in Mom's neck, with its familiar lemony smell, and hear her say that these problems would all go away. . . . The only problem was that Mom *was* the problem. Joss curled herself into a ball. The lights in the dorm windows across from the pond grew brighter and brighter as darkness fell. The air was a little too crisp now, and her sweaty clothes felt moldy and damp against her skin. No matter. She wouldn't go home. She'd die of exposure before—

The crackling of twigs from the opposite end of the island snapped Joss' thoughts. Just a bird hopping around. The noises came closer. In spite of herself, Joss was frightened. The glowing path of a flashlight was now only a few yards away. If she screamed, who would hear her? She tried to press herself into the ground and think like a rock.

"Okay, we've got you surrounded. Come on out. With your hands up!" The voice sounded familiar, like a third-rate imitation of John Wayne's.

Joss sat bolt upright. "Fletcher!" she cried out in a loud voice.

There was a crash as the flashlight dropped, and for a split second its beam was trained on Fletcher's equally startled face.

"Oh God! You scared me. You really *are* out here." Fletcher bent down for his flashlight and recovered himself. "I mean, I had a hunch, but I wasn't sure." He smiled a goofy, self-conscious smile. "Your mother called a little while ago. Asking if I knew where you were. She sounded upset and said if I heard from you to *please* have you call home. . . . I don't know. The way she was talking, I could tell she didn't think anything bad had happened. Like an accident. It was more like she thought you didn't *want* to come home. I have to admit that was pretty hard to picture, you pulling a stunt like running away. But I said to myself, 'If Joss was going to run away, where would she go?' Then it hit me. The island was just the sort of dippy place you'd pick." The obvious pleasure Fletcher was getting from his shrewd deductions rankled Joss.

"I can live without the sarcasm, Sherlock," she said. "In case you don't remember, officially you and I are not on speaking terms." Joss stared straight at Fletcher. "It's just like you to cut me dead for weeks and now to start acting as if absolutely nothing has happened."

Fletcher looked a little surprised. He held up a hand, a peace gesture. "Okay, okay. Don't get sore, Joss. But after I bothered coming all the way out here to see if you were all right, the least you can do is tell me what's going on."

"I'll tell you. But first you tell me what's been going on with you."

Fletcher just sat fiddling with the switch on his flashlight. "Would you believe temporary insanity?" he said finally.

Joss shook her head. "Sorry, Fletcher, but you're going to have to do better than that." Then she added more kindly, "If you want to be friends again, I need to know."

196

For a moment Fletcher sat silently, hunched over, playing with one of the laces of his sneakers. "Okay, here goes," he said, his face hidden almost entirely in shadow. "When I said temporary insanity before, I was joking. But in a way that's really what it was like. For a while it seemed as if all I could think about was sex."

"You're telling *me*?" Joss couldn't resist saying.

"It wasn't any fun for me either, Jocelyn," Fletcher said defensively. "It was horrible, as a matter of fact. You won't believe this, but even during that test in French we had a couple of weeks ago, I was going nuts. The way Fein was sitting, I could sort of see up her skirt."

"Madame Fein was turning you *on*?" It was impossible for Joss to keep the shock from her voice. Besides the killer breath, Madame Fein had a bristly mustache and practically predated the French Revolution.

"Listen, you don't have to tell me. I *know* how perverted it was. I felt like I belonged on a psycho ward. But I'm trying to explain. Anything female got to me." Fletcher paused. "You included."

Joss wasn't sure how she felt about being lumped in the same category with Madame Fein, but she remained silent and let Fletcher continue.

"Suddenly you weren't just *you* anymore. You were also a girl. Maybe because I spent the most time with you, I thought about you the most. I don't know. But I even started dreaming about you. I felt awful. One night I had this really wild dream where this motorcycle gang kidnaped both of us and made us take off all our clothes and then they wanted us to—"

"It's okay, Fletcher," Joss interrupted quickly. "You can spare me the gory details."

"Anyway, that day in the attic when we were alone, all I could think about was how I had never even kissed anyone and how at the rate I was going, I would probably be thirty before I did. All of a sudden I started getting this desperate feeling, like it was now or never, and then . . . well the rest, you know. I felt like such a creep after. Plus my feelings were hurt. . . . I just kept wishing everything could go back to the way it used to be. But I knew it couldn't. And somehow I blamed you for that." Fletcher looked up at Joss tentatively, waiting for a reply.

Fletcher, Joss knew, would have come right back with a flip remark to show that everything was okay. Perhaps he would have nodded solemnly and said, "I can really relate to that," *à la* Dr. Dwoskin. But Fletcher's style wasn't hers. Not really.

"I'm really glad you came, Fletcher" was all Joss finally murmured. "Honest I am. I can't tell you how cruddy I've felt ever since that day." She wanted to take Fletcher by his underdeveloped shoulders and hug him hard. But she didn't. She figured it would just embarrass both of them. And it struck Joss that Fletcher was right. It never would be quite the same. From now on they'd always be a little careful around each other.

Fletcher acknowledged her with a curt nod. Then he said, "Okay, now that I finished spilling out my guts, it's your turn. And this better be good. *Duck Soup* is on tonight, and I'm missing the whole thing."

Fair was fair, Joss conceded to herself, and anyway, it might be a relief to pour out the whole story. As long as Fletcher didn't blab to anybody, and something told Joss he wouldn't.

"Come on, kid. Out with it." Fletcher was now doing his Jimmy Cagney. "I haven't got all day."

Joss took a deep breath. "Okay, but you're not going to believe this. Mom—" Joss stopped, searching for the least horrible way of putting it. "Mom has been seeing another man."

It took a second for Joss' words to penetrate. A moment before, Fletcher had had this skeptical, impatient look on his face, as if he expected Joss to come out with something really lame. Now his mouth dropped open, but nothing came out. It was the first time Joss had ever seen Fletcher look genuinely flabbergasted.

"You've got to be putting me on," he said at last. "*Your* mother?"

"I know how incredible it sounds," Joss said miserably. "But it's true." And she proceeded to fill in all the bits of circumstantial evidence leading up to the phone conversation she'd interrupted. "All along I thought Daddy was the one who wanted to leave. I thought *he* was in love with Phoebe Jackson."

"Your mother and Professor *Macdunna*!" It was difficult to tell what shocked Fletcher more, Mom's infidelity or the fact that Professor Macdunna turned out to be the man in question. Joss knew what Fletcher must be thinking. Why, next to Daddy, Professor Macdunna was a joke. How could Mom possibly even think about kissing— Joss stopped herself. She refused to think about that part of it. If she did, she'd go nuts.

"At least it seems like whatever was going on is all over," Fletcher tried to comfort her.

"Yes, and now we can go back to being the perfect happy little family we've always been. Right?"

"I'm sorry, Joss. I don't know what else to say."

"It's okay. I'm just pissed at myself for being such a twit." Joss shivered. A sudden breeze had blown up, ruffling the calm surface of the pond and rustling through the weeping willow trees.

Fletcher stood up. "Come on, Joss. Time to go. You can't stay here all night. It's starting to get cold."

"All right." Joss rose sullenly. "But I'm not going home."

"You could stay over at my house tonight."

"No!" What would they tell Fletcher's parents? The thought of Dr. Dwoskin's long, questioning looks was more than Joss could bear.

"Well, Laura won't be back from Boston until tomorrow, so I don't know what else to suggest . . . unless you really want to run away. Then you could hitch to Times Square and become a teenage hooker. Who knows? They might even make a made-for-TV movie about you."

"Very funny." Joss made a weak face. Then she scooped up a handful of pebbles and began chucking them, one by one, into the water. Finally she looked at Fletcher. "Fletcher, what am I going to do? What am I going to say to Ma?" Joss couldn't help it. Suddenly tears started running down her cheeks and into her mouth.

Fletcher patted Joss awkwardly on the shoulder. "I don't know. But sooner or later you have to face her." Then he went over to his canoe, pushed it down into the water, motioned Joss to get in hers, and they both paddled back to shore.

The moment Joss turned the front door to her house, she realized how angry she was. Mom came rushing toward her, her arms outstretched, her bathrobe flying about her, ready to envelop her. But Joss ducked aside quickly. If she hadn't, she was sure she would have shoved Mom away.

Daddy was standing in the hallway, looking tired and nervous. "I'm so glad you're home," he said. "I suppose I will now make a not very discreet exit." And, after kissing Joss lightly on the forehead, he went upstairs.

Now they were alone. She and Mom.

"Come into the kitchen," her mother said softly. There on the table, awaiting her arrival, was a tall glass of ginger ale and a plate of toast with the crusts cut off. It was what Mom always fixed when she got sick.

How pathetic. Joss pressed her lips together in a disgusted grimace. Did Mom actually expect that this would make her feel any better? Kiss the boo-boo and make it go away.

"Please, Joss. Sit down." Mom took a cigarette from a pack of Daddy's Pall Malls lying on the table and struck a match. She smoked three, maybe four times a year, and the way she took such short little puffs and placed the cigarette right in the center of her mouth always made her look like a kid who was just learning how.

"I'll discuss this with you once. But then not again, ever. Understood?" Mom said shakily.

Joss glared at the toast and soda. Who was Mom to be setting down rules, anyway? She was the one who had broken them.

"Does Daddy know?" Joss asked. She tried to keep her voice steady. The answer just had to be yes. Otherwise how could they all possibly live in the same house keeping that kind of secret? She'd never be able to look at Daddy in the face again. Never!

Her mother nodded slowly, tapping her cigarette nervously into an ashtray. "I told him everything yesterday—our anniversary. Not great timing, I suppose." She sighed. "But I couldn't keep it to myself any longer. . . . He'd known, suspected anyway, for a while before that. . . ."

Joss remembered yesterday in their room. The two of them talking so seriously. Mom crying. It made more sense now. And Daddy's card too, where he asked her to stay with him.

"So?" For the first time Joss attempted to look at Mom full face. "Are you planning to pack up and leave for England, or what?"

Mom's face crumpled. Good. Joss wanted to hurt her. She wanted to make her feel miserable.

"Joss!" Mom's voice rose an octave. "You heard me on the phone. It's over. Besides, I never ever considered leaving *you*!" Mom fumbled for Joss' hand, but Joss yanked it away before bursting into tears.

"How could you?" Joss wailed. "I don't understand. I don't understand *anything*."

Suddenly her mother was kneeling next to her, hugging her, brushing away the hair that had fallen into Joss' eyes, making soothing sounds. Joss gave in. She felt like clutching onto Mom for dear life.

"I thought you loved Daddy so much," she managed to croak out. "Didn't you always tell me how you fell in love with him at first sight?"

"I was *nineteen* then." Mom drew back a little from Joss, held her by the shoulders, and looked into her face. "I know that sounds old to you, but it isn't. I was still a child. Daddy seemed so worldly-wise to me. He was all of twenty-three." Mom smiled. "I could almost laugh when I think about it."

"Don't you still love Daddy?" *Please. Please say you do*, Joss thought.

"I suppose I must. Otherwise I don't think I could

203

stay. But I feel Daddy treats me as if I'm still nineteen and a hick from the midwest who's not as smart or as accomplished as he is." Mom rubbed her eyes and then squeezed the bridge of her nose as if she had a bad headache. "Joss, everyone wants to feel special. Daddy just hasn't been doing that for me."

"And Professor Macdunna was?" Joss let that slip. She had told herself she would never so much as utter his name.

"Yes, he did." Mom stood and lit another Pall Mall. "But that's not something I want to go into. Even if I could explain how I felt, I wouldn't. But I hope you'll understand that what happened didn't happen because I wanted it to." Her mother was sounding just like Fletcher now. He'd said the same thing, he couldn't help how he'd acted. Was everyone really at the mercy of their feelings? It was scary.

"People can be important to you in different ways at different times," Mom went on. "Does that make any sense to you?"

Joss shrugged her shoulders. Nothing made much sense. Not at this moment at least.

"Listen to me, Joss. Daddy and I want to try to make things work. That's all I can promise." Mom bent down again and kissed Joss on the forehead. There was a halo of tobacco smoke surrounding her, and the smell was unfamiliar, off-putting. But Mom after all was still Mom. "I love you so much," she whispered. "And I'm so sorry to have hurt you."

A little while later, Mom tucked Joss into bed, as

if she was six again, and turned out the light. It was still pretty early—not even ten o'clock—but Joss felt as if she had been up for two days straight. She fell asleep almost instantly.

That night she dreamed she was at a fancy dress ball. Later all she could remember were snatches, shreds of the dream, but she knew she had been wearing the Alice Blue Gown and everyone was there—her parents, Fletcher and Laura, Twig, Professor Macdunna. Even Weezie. Glittering crystal chandeliers hung from the ceiling, and while the orchestra played, the guests spun about the floor, making a beautiful, intricate, kaleidoscopic pattern. Never the same. Always changing. Joss was unsure of the steps. At times she felt she was being whisked off her feet. She could not even see who her partner was. All the same, she was part of the dance.

Afterward

"Eat up, folks. The movie goes on at two ten."

"Fletcher! We've still got almost half an hour!" Laura said, taking another sip of her soda.

"But what if there's a line?"

Twig snorted. "A line? You've got to be kidding!" He stood up. "I'm getting some more pizza. Anybody want anything?"

"No, thanks. I'm fine," Joss answered.

As soon as Twig was up at the counter, Fletcher leaned over and said conspiratorially to Joss, "So? How am I doing? I'm being really nice, aren't I?" He looked at Laura for confirmation. "Admit it. I'm being a real prince."

"Fletcher! Will you kindly shut up!" Joss whispered.

"Twig is going to hear you." In her panic, Joss spit out a tiny glob of pizza cheese. It landed on her T-shirt, forming a neat dime-sized grease spot on her chest. "Oh, now look!" Joss wailed. Then she caught herself and continued in a low, furious voice. "I knew this little outing was a mistake."

"Relax, Joss," Laura counseled in a soothing voice. "It's just a double date. We're going to have a good time."

Joss smiled weakly. It was hard enough being around Twig. Now not only was Fletcher watching her every move, but three booths down Bobo and Michelle were huddled together, whispering and cracking up every two seconds. If they *were* laughing about the four of them, Joss knew it was purely sour grapes on Bobo's part. Even so, it made her self-conscious. Plus Joss was afraid of joking too much with Fletcher in case Laura might feel left out or Twig might get the wrong idea and think she was more interested in Fletcher than him. Oh God! It was all so complicated.

Joss sighed and tried to rearrange her face into a cheerier expression as Twig headed back toward their booth. Lately it seemed to her she didn't know how to act around *anybody*. Home was certainly no easier. Mom and Daddy were so strange around each other still. Especially Daddy. He treated Mom as if she was getting over some long, terrible disease.

Right after Daddy had gotten tenure, her parents had gone away to New York City for a weekend. Just the two of them. It was supposed to be a celebration. After all the worrying, tenure at last. But it seemed so anticlimactic. When they left, both Mom and Daddy had looked so tired and wrung out, all Joss could imagine them doing was sleeping in their hotel room for four days straight.

How weird it all was. On the one hand, nothing had really changed. Mom and Daddy were still together; they'd be staying in Higham after all; she and Fletcher were friends. Yet everything was different.

Twig slid into the booth beside Joss. He was juggling three more buckling slices of pizza and a giant soda. That was another thing she loved about Twig. Next to him, she ate like a bird.

Joss watched him chew and began to feel happier. Even his Adam's apple, bobbing up and down as he swallowed, looked beautiful to her.

"You know, this is the first time this movie has been shown since it came out in 1956," Fletcher informed the group.

"Must be a real gem," Joss muttered.

"A 3-D movie about killer spiders! Come on!" Fletcher exclaimed. "It was obviously an idea ahead of its time."

"I just hope it isn't too gory," Laura said. "I hate movies when they're too gory."

"Good luck!" Twig said. "Killer spiders in 3-D. Somehow I *don't* think we're going to watch them spinning webs."

All the way to the movie theater, Joss worried about whether or not she was supposed to pay. At Phil's, without even thinking, she had handed $1.25 to the counter guy for her slice of pizza and Coke, but Twig had given her a funny look. Had that been wrong? Should she have just stood there, waiting for Twig to fork over the money? It was too bad this dating business didn't have definite rules. It was all so unclear.

When they reached the Buster Keaton, where *Black Widow* was playing, Joss decided the best strategy was to position herself slightly behind Twig as they went up for their tickets.

"Two, please," he told the ticket seller.

"Uh—would you like some money, Twig?" Joss couldn't help volunteering.

"No, I wouldn't," he answered flatly.

Why hadn't she kept her big mouth shut? Now Twig was mad.

Joss followed him inside the lobby, where an usher was passing out pairs of 3-D glasses. Laura tried hers on.

"How do I look?" she giggled.

"Very punk," Joss said.

"Really," Twig agreed. "This is going to be great." He got some popcorn, then motioned to Joss and headed for the center aisle.

"No, let's sit upstairs," Fletcher said. Upstairs was the make-out section. Everybody knew that.

Laura smiled widely. "Okay by me."

Twig shrugged, and they all trooped up to seats in the first row behind the railing. Except for a couple who were miles away up by the projection booth, not a soul was around.

"And you thought it would be crowded," Twig said to Fletcher, as they settled into their seats. Fletcher was farthest in, with Laura next to him, then Joss, and last, Twig on the aisle. Already Laura was leaning to her left, snuggling up against Fletcher. Joss remained rigid in her seat, staring straight ahead at the kaleidoscope image on the screen. Twig was hunkered down in his seat, his feet propped up against the railing in front of them. Every so often he passed the bucket of popcorn over to her, then took a handful for himself, tossing the kernels into his mouth, one by one.

The opening credits rolled by on the screen. Joss tried to get comfortable too and concentrate on the movie, although she couldn't help noticing Fletcher's arm draped around Laura's shoulder. Boy, he sure wasn't wasting any time!

The movie took place in a science lab with all the actors and actresses rushing around in long white coats like doctors, carrying clipboards. It seemed they were performing a top-secret experiment on a black widow spider, injecting it with something called cerebellin to make it more intelligent. The spider, huge, black, and hairy, was kept in the laboratory in a small, flimsy-looking cage.

"Ooh, look!" Laura squealed. There was a close-up of the black widow, waving its hairy arms through the little bars of its cage.

"It really looks like its arms are coming straight out at you!" Joss marveled.

Twig whispered to her, "Yeah, almost feels like that spider could come crawling up and tickle you. Right here!" Twig got her in the ribs, good and hard.

"Cut it out!" Joss yelped, laughing. She swatted at Twig and sent the bucket of popcorn flying over the railing.

"Hey, who's the joker up there?" someone in the audience yelled from below.

"Now see what you made me do!" Joss giggled and gave Twig another swat.

"Will you two stop acting like babies. We're going to get kicked out," Fletcher warned. Joss knew it was Fletcher from the voice. Otherwise it would have been hard to tell which of the two figures, huddled so closely together, had spoken.

"All right, all right. We'll be good," Twig promised. He squeezed Joss' hand as if they were accomplices in some crime. Then instead of letting go, he kept on holding her hand, on the armrest between their seats.

Joss reddened. Had Fletcher and Laura noticed what had happened? No. They were too busy with each other. Joss moved closer to Twig and squeezed his hand back. His fingers felt soft and warm, and even a while later, when her hand had begun to grow all numb and prickly, Joss didn't move a muscle. She figured she'd stay this way until her whole arm got gangrene and fell off if that's the way Twig wanted it.

All of a sudden the music in the movie got louder. A scary part was coming.

A pretty research assistant was alone in the lab with one of the older scientists. They were kissing each other feverishly, and, of course, neither one of them noticed that the tiny door to the spider's cage was open.

"Oh! Oh! Dr. Carstairs. We shouldn't be here. This is wrong. I'm a married woman," the research assistant cried as the spider crept silently along the counter top right behind them.

Laura started shrieking.

Joss let out a little gasp. But not from fear. She scrunched down in her seat and waited for the sick hollow feeling in her stomach to pass. It came whenever something reminded her of Mom and Professor Macdunna. And so *much* reminded her of Mom and Professor Macdunna.

It seemed the harder she tried *not* to think about the whole mess, the more it sneaked up on her and caught her by surprise.

The whole mess. Joss didn't know what else to call it.

"Face it, Joss. Your mother had an affair," Fletcher had stated the other day. "She isn't the first person in the world, you know."

"But *affair* would mean they—they were doing it,"

Joss had countered. "And I'm not a hundred percent sure they were."

Fletcher had smacked his forehead in disbelief. "Of course they were doing it. I mean, I don't want to make you feel worse than you do, Joss, but do you actually believe they were just holding hands?"

"Oh, probably you're right," Joss said with a sigh. Only she kept remembering what Weezie had said about people and attachments. Couldn't her mother have cared for the professor in a special way? A different way?

Late at night, lying in bed, Joss would go over and over all the things Mom had said to her that night. And all the things she hadn't said. Joss felt that if she could only get it straight in her mind what had actually gone on, then she could lay the matter to rest. But she knew, too, that what really mattered now was not so much Mom and the professor but Mom and Daddy. . . . About the most she could do was keep her fingers crossed.

Halfway through the picture, just after one of the scientists had been bitten by the black widow and was writhing around on the floor, Twig kissed Joss.

It took her completely by surprise. One minute she'd been watching the movie and then—whammo!—there he was, the taste of buttered popcorn still on his breath, his 3-D glasses pressing into her face.

Once she got over her surprise, Joss settled into the business at hand, and for the next half hour she forgot about everything except Twig.

It was incredible, Joss thought to herself, how many different kinds of kisses there were—soft ones, long ones, wet ones, ones where you moved your mouth around a whole lot. And Twig was good at all of them.

Joss smiled happily to herself as they started in on another long, moving-around one. So this was it—true love! So far it was turning out to be everything it was cracked up to be.

Way too soon, the movie ended and the lights came back on in the theater.

They all disentangled themselves and removed their glasses. Laura patted her hair. Fletcher blinked. Twig coughed self-consciously.

"What'd I tell you. Great flick, huh?" Fletcher said.

Outside the movie house, Fletcher and Laura and Twig and Joss split off in two directions.

"See you Monday," Fletcher called to them. Laura looked back over her shoulder and waved. Joss watched them turn the corner, hand in hand.

"They really like each other," Joss said to Twig. It was still so strange. Thinking of Fletcher as part of a couple.

"Yeah, they do," Twig said as they started toward Joss' house. "I always thought that you and Fletcher were—you know. I always thought you and Fletcher sort of had a thing for each other."

Joss smiled and shook her head. "We're just good friends is all. I think Fletcher is great but not that way. There's only one person I feel that way about."

Twig got the message. "Oh yeah? Well, me, too!"

he said, clamping an arm around Joss' shoulder.

When they reached her front door, Joss said, "My parents are home, but if you want, you can come in."

Twig shook his head. "I'd better get going. A big family night tonight. We're all driving to my aunt's in Medwin for dinner."

"Well . . . thanks for today, Twig. It was great." Joss was leaning against the front door facing him.

Twig nodded. Then he bent over slightly, his hand resting on the door over Joss' head, and kissed her. A soft, dry, quick one. "Uh, maybe I'll call you tomorrow. To see how you're doing." Then Twig started down the front walk.

Joss waved to Twig, even though he couldn't see her, before going inside. Then she watched him from the front hall window—Twig with that loose, easy, jocky walk of his—until he disappeared down Willow Street.

"That you, honey?" her mother called from the kitchen. The sweet smell of banana bread baking filled the house.

"Yeah, it's me, Ma," Joss answered dreamily.

"There's a letter for you on the front hall table."

The envelope was postmarked Deerfield. Joss tore it open.

"Dear Joss," Weezie had written, "I came across this picture and thought you might like to have it. People are such a mystery, don't you think? And thank God for that, I say!"

It was a small formal portrait showing Millie and

Elliot standing together, very prim. Millie's hair was piled up in a topknot and Elliot was clutching a straw boater in one hand. At first Joss couldn't imagine why Weezie had bothered to send the photograph. Joss hadn't even opened Millie's diary once since that day she'd biked out to Deerfield.

Joss started to stick the photo back in the envelope when she took a closer look. This time she noticed that while Elliot was staring straight ahead at the camera, Millie's face was turned ever so slightly toward his and she seemed to be holding back a smile. Then Joss caught another detail. Millie and Elliot were holding hands! Very inconspicuously, these proper New Englanders. But there they were.

What did it mean? Had Millie loved nerdy Elliot after all? Joss shook her head and smiled a puzzled smile. Weezie was right, she supposed. People were a mystery. It was so hard to tell about anybody. About all you could do, Joss guessed, was be sure to look closely.

Also in Puffin Plus

ONE MORE RIVER   *Lynne Reid Banks*
THE WRITING ON THE WALL   *Lynne Reid Banks*
EASY CONNECTIONS   *Liz Berry*
THE WONDERFUL STORY OF HENRY SUGAR
Roald Dahl
ARE YOU LISTENING, KAREN?   *David Day*
HEALER   *Peter Dickinson*
THE SUMMER AFTER THE FUNERAL   *Jane Gardam*
SUMMER OF MY GERMAN SOLDIER   *Bette Greene*
EDITH JACKSON   *Rosa Guy*
THE DISAPPEARANCE   *Rosa Guy*
THE ENDLESS STEPPE   *Esther Hautzig*
NO PLACE LIKE   *Gene Kemp*
THE FORTUNATE FEW   *Tim Kennemore*
MISCHLING, SECOND DEGREE   *Ilse Koehn*
THE ENNEAD   *Jan Mark*
JACOB HAVE I LOVED   *Katherine Paterson*
AN OPEN MIND   *Susan Sallis*
LET THE CIRCLE BE UNBROKEN   *Mildred D.-Taylor*